26/6/25
30/6/25

My Vice Is Your Unfathomable Agony

My Vice Is Your Unfathomable Agony
First Edition October 2023
Edited By: Christine Morgan and Judith Sonnet
Formatted By: Stephen Cooper
Cover Illustration By: Christy Aldridge
(Grim Poppy Design)

Copyright © 2023 Otis Bateman

My Vice Is Your Unfathomable Agony

By Otis Bateman

Contents

!!TRIGGER WARNING!!

This book contains graphic violence and sexual depravity. This is meant to be horrific in every way possible; consider this your goddamned trigger warning...

Dedication

This one is for the gang: Judith Sonnet, Brian G. Berry, Christina Aldridge, Stephen Cooper, Erica Summers, and Meghin Uhl

Also, this is dedicated to the people who forgot how good I am at gore and depravity… Maybe you'll remember my name again.

Special shoutout to Christine Morgan for taking over editing duties and for Stephen Cooper for all of his additional help with formatting and for being there whenever I needed a pep talk or word of encouragement! In the immortal words of The Golden Girls, thank you for being a friend!

XXXtra special thanks to Judith Sonnet for the extra pair of eyes and second edit! You're the best!

Quotes

"Please don't confuse my misanthropy for misogyny."
— Chandler Morrison, Dead Inside

"People who hunt other people for a vocation. All we want to talk about is what it's like. Shit that went down. The entire fucked-upness of it. It's not easy butchering people it's hard work. Physically and mentally it's hard work. People don't realize, you need to vent." — Edmund Kemper, Serial Killer

"I explore my thoughts through murder, devoting my life to mutilation."
— Cannibal Corpse

"We'll be remembered more for what we destroy than what we create."
— Chuck Palahniuk, Invisible Monsters

"I like to dissect girls. Did you know I'm utterly insane?"
— Bret Easton Ellis, American Psycho

Chapter 1

The Job

The headlights from the Peterbilt 379 tractor trailer illuminate the dark and winding road heading back to the trucking facility. Justin Fuller had gone out of his way to deliver one last load for the night before calling it a day. His trailer was jam-packed full of DVD players, which were supposedly going to make VCR's absolute relics. But with prices starting at six-hundred dollars and topping off at one-thousand dollars, Justin wasn't too sure about this new innovation in technology just yet. He thought he'd be sticking with his videocassettes for the foreseeable future.

When he arrived at the electronics retailer, they were inexplicably closed, forcing him to return to work with the merchandise still in tow. Hopefully tomorrow he could just re-deliver the players bright and early so he could empty his truck and get back to earning a wage. His fiancée Nancy Lochiano's father had gotten him on at Comet Trucking even though Justin really didn't have any experience in the trucking industry.

Justin had heard things about Nancy's father Rossario. Low murmurs about him being a big-time mob boss and such. Justin had only seen the good side of Rossario though. He loved his daughter and he had taken to Justin quickly as well. Sometimes, fathers would hate the male suitors wanting to be with their daughters, but Justin never got that inclination from him. Rossario just generally wanted his daughter to be happy, hooking Justin up with such a lucrative trade to try and make the young couple's life financially easier from the jump.

As the massive truck drove through the night, Justin hummed along with the song playing on the radio. *Semi-Charmed Life,* by Third Eye Blind. He was getting tired; it had been a very long day and all he wanted to do was eat some supper, take a shower, and fall asleep in front of the boob tube to his favorite series, *Buffy the Vampire Slayer*.

He took an especially hairpin turn with an acute inner angle, making it necessary to turn the lumbering vehicle about 180° to continue on the road. As he corrected the big rig and the road straightened out, Justin was shocked to see an obstruction. A man was lying face down on the blacktop ahead of him. Nearby, a young child–probably ten–was waving his hands frantically toward the encroaching truck. Trying to catch Justin's attention so he didn't run them over!" Justin instinctively slammed on the brakes, causing the behemoth truck to fishtail on the dampened road and swerve haphazardly onto the shoulder of the two-lane street, just missing the two bodies by a mere fraction of an inch. He screeched in terror, sweat carpeting his pale, trembling face, having narrowly missed the little boy and the unflinching man.

Tubthumping, by Chumbawamba, played softly in the otherwise deathly silent cab of Justin's truck. The upbeat, happy tempo of the song was a total oxymoron for the sheer alarm that Justin had gone through in a matter of seconds.

"Jesus fucking Christ!" Justin cried.

He took a moment to compose himself before he jumped out of the truck to check on the kid and the prone body in the road. The child appeared abysmal; besides looking terrified, his whole body was damp from the light misting of rain that had been falling for hours. His fat cheeks were bright pink from the nipping cold.

Justin knelt so that he could look at the boy eye to eye before he addressed him properly.

"What's your name, son? What's happening? Who's that?" Justin asked in rapid fire succession.

For a moment, the boy said nothing at all. Then, like a stubborn cork being withdrawn from a bottle, the boy began to spew out a quick barrage of words.

"Our car broke down mister and when my daddy and me got out of his car he grabbed his chest and fell right there on the road! I tried my best to wake him up, but I couldn't! I'm scared that he died!" The kid sobbed.

"Okay, first things first, what's your name, son?"

"AJ, sir."

"No need to call me sir; my name is Justin. Nice to meet you, AJ. Now, I'm going to go check on your daddy… what is his name?"

"His name is Brandon, mister… I mean Justin. You think he is going to be alright?"

For a moment, Justin was silent. He didn't want to fill the boy with false hope if there wasn't any. Of course, he wasn't a doctor, but he could at least check the body and see if he could administer any sort of aid for him.

"Well AJ, I'll give your dad a quick look over, okay?"

AJ nodded in response, his sniffles the only audible rebuttal given. Justin crept over to the downed man and prepared to get a better sense of what precisely had happened to him. As he stooped and turned over the incapacitated body of AJ's father, he was finally able to see Brandon's visage. He was not prepared to see the man smiling back at him maliciously. Startled, Justin quickly backtracked, only to feel the barrel of a gun being jammed painfully into the small of his back.

"What the–" Justin began, before being struck in his temple from the butt of the gun, dropping him instantly.

"Man, we got you mister! You totally fell for it, dummy!" AJ cackled cruelly.

Dazedly, Justin looked around, taking in his surroundings. He was now encircled by three staring faces. A third man had entered the fray, the one who had struck him with the gun. Justin felt extremely lightheaded, and his precious life fluid surged down the side of his face from the violent blow.

"What's happening?" he slurred.

The butt of the gun once again cracked down, causing brilliant pain to display a fireworks explosion in his mind.

"Well, Justin, it's simple what's happening. We're going to rob you and take your truck and everything inside of it," Brandon said. He cast a smug, caustic grin at his newly discovered accomplice. "Does that sound about right to you Christopher? Is that what we're doing?"

"That sounds about perfect! We're about to get paid in DVD players!"

Even though Justin had just been assaulted and struck in his head twice, the fact that one of the robbers knew the exact contents of his cargo did not go unnoticed.

Justin immediately thought of Stephen Cooper, a loader that worked on the dock at Comet Trucking. He had made it a point to strike up a conversation with Justin earlier and inquire about what he was hauling. Justin had always thought Stephen was a genuine piece of shit, and now this cemented it.

He looked at the two men before turning a pleading glance at AJ. The expression quickly evaporated once he saw the child's malevolent elation over the entire situation.

"Don't look at me like that, mister, 'cuz I don't give a shit 'bout you! My daddy said I get ta keep one of the movie players if I tricked ya! So . . . I DID! We got ya good, didn't we?" AJ laughed.

The others quickly followed suit with the gleeful bad seed, laughing heartily at Justin's expense like they were watching an incredibly hilarious sitcom. Justin began to cry in earnest. He thought of his beautiful, young fiancée Nancy, and of the baby that was growing daily in her belly, and wondered if he would even see the day of his wedding or the birth of his first child. Maybe if he didn't try to be a cowboy and let them just take the truck, they would let him go back to his life. He would have a few lumps on his head, but at least he would be alive!

His tongue darted out quickly, wetting his dry, chapped lips as he prepared to plead his case to the muggers.

"Now look, this has gone on just about far enough. Feel free to take my truck and everything that is in it. I won't stand in your way, and I won't alert the authorities until after you've gone. Shit, I'll even tell them you all were wearing masks, and I couldn't make any of you out! I won't even mention the boy!"

They looked at him like he was a decrepit old man in the throes of severe dementia. All three slowly shook their heads "*no*" in unison.

"Sorry man, but we can't let you live. I think if you try and look at it from our perspective, you'll understand."

Justin was about to say something else in a desperate attempt to stave off his possible death when he felt the cold muzzle of the pistol being placed against his head. Before he could utter a single word in his defense, the absurdly loud report was all encompassing. Justin barely had time to understand what was happening. He felt an immediate agonizing pain, and then it was gone.

What also was gone was the entire right quadrant of his skull.

The bullet ripped through flesh, bone, and hair, belching out a spray of gore into the crisp night air.

Justin fell heavily to the asphalt face first, crushing the cartilage in his nose and splitting his lips open in the process. His rapidly depleting blood fanned out onto the road. His hammering heart continued to pump erratically as he went through the final throes of death. His mouth spasmed grotesquely as he took his last gasps of life-giving oxygen.

His hazy thoughts went to Nancy and their unborn child. If it were to be a boy, Gavin would've been a good name.

A brittle smile etched across Justin's bloody face as he succumbed to the massive blood loss.

***

Brandon and Christopher dragged the corpse into a dense patch of foliage, not bothering with the effort to bury it properly or even attempting to hide it well.

"Once me and AJ take this truck to the drop off point and get paid," Brandon said, "come pick us up in the car, and then let's go to TJ's Diner. My treat!"

"I do love their giant tenderloins!" Christopher laughed.

"I want chocolate chip pancakes!" AJ announced.

"You can get whatever you like, buddy!" Brandon said.

"And don't forget my DVD player. I really fooled that doofus, didn't I?" AJ snickered.

"You sure did, and you're definitely getting a DVD player; I couldn't have pulled off the job without you," Brandon said, ruffling his son's messy hair affectionately.

"Can I honk the horn, too, Dad?"

"Of course, you can!"

"Alright ramblers, let's get to rambling!" Christopher said.

***

No one thought of the dead trucker as they drove away from the premises, assuming he was just a lowly blue-collar worker of no vital importance.

They couldn't have been more mistaken …

Chapter 2

Sifting Out the Truth

When Justin didn't come home, Nancy made a frantic, late-night call to her father.

Rossario Lochiano groggily pawed for the telephone beside his nightstand, toppling over the glass of water resting nearby in the process.

"Goddammit!"

He grabbed the phone from the cradle and barked menacingly into the receiver.

"What do you want, and it better be good!"

"Daddy? I'm sorry I called so late --"

"Sweetie? I'm so sorry! I didn't realize it was you."

"Daddy, Justin still hasn't come home, and that's not like him at all!" Nancy cried.

"Slow down and start from the beginning."

Nancy took some deep breaths. After she finished telling her father all that she knew, Rossario promised her he would get to the bottom of it immediately.

When they hung up, Rossario -- who happened to be not only the young mother-to-be's father but also the Don of the Kansas City mafia -- got back on the phone. He called his capos Sal, Vito, and Paulie, and brought them all up to speed on what his daughter had just relayed to him.

They arrived shortly to pick him up and headed to Comet Trucking to speak with the night supervisor, Jimmy DiMeo.

After the two shook hands, Rossario got right down to brass tacks.

"Look Jimmy, my daughter is freaking out about Justin not making it home. Have you heard anything about him or his whereabouts tonight?"

"Well, Mr. Lochiano, he had a huge truckload of DVD players he was supposed to deliver to an electronics store over in North Kansas City, but they were closed when he got there. So, he got on the CB radio and let me know that he was going to have to try and redeliver the product tomorrow. I told him that was fine, to bring the merchandise back to the terminal, and just try again in the morning. I haven't heard anything since, but he should have been back by now."

Rossario, already wondering if Justin had been set up by an inside man, posed the next question as innocuously as possible.

"So, besides you, would anyone else be privy to Justin's route or the freight that was in his trailer?"

Jimmy thought about it for a moment or two. "I suppose Stephen Cooper, since he's the one who sets up the delivery routes for all the drivers."

The cogs in Rossario's brain whirred into high gear, putting two and two together in seconds.

"Do you happen to have Stephen's address, Jimmy?" Rossario asked.

"Let me go into the office and get that for you, sir."

As he went upstairs, Rossario turned to his cohorts.

"When we get this fuck's address, we are going to pay his ass a visit, and get the full story. I'd bet my life savings he sold that kid out to someone so they could boost that truck."

"Yeah, most definitely, boss," Paulie said. "I've heard about this Cooper fuck; he'd sell his own mother out if it benefited his weaselly ass!"

"We'll get the truth outta him," Vito smirked. "I've got some items in my trunk that, how should I say this, will expedite the truth from his no-good dicksucking, lying mouth."

"I just hope your girl's fiancé is alright," Sal added.

Rossario had a sinking feeling in his gut that he knew not to ignore. Being the Don of the KC mafia, he had learned a long time ago to trust his instincts, as they had yet to steer him wrong. He had a feeling that the nice young man his daughter planned to marry was probably dead but would hold out a smidgen of hope for just a bit longer, until they forced the truth out of this snake mother fucker Stephen Cooper.

"Sorry about the wait," Jimmy said as he returned. "HR just has shit everywhere in their office. It took me a minute figuring out their filing system!"

"No worries, Jimmy," Rossario assured him. "I know we're keeping you from your real work. We'll be out of your hair in a minute."

"Oh, it's no problem, it's an honor to do a favor for you, sir!"

"No need for that sir shit, paisan; just call me Rossario!"

Jimmy smiled broadly in response. Rossario never tired of the respect constantly heaped upon him. A lot of it stemmed from his good nature and humble attitude, rather than the usual fear and intimidation factors. Rossario was a tough but fair boss, but he was never arrogant, and that attribute endured him to most people.

"Here's Stephen's address. Hopefully he will have some more answers for you."

"I have a strong feeling he will, Jimmy; thanks for your assistance." Rossario said.

***

Stephen was half-dozing in his La-Z-Boy recliner, with a porno playing in his VCR: *Edward Penishands*, an XXX parody of the popular Tim Burton film. He had probably watched it twenty times already. Not only was it funny, but it was also hot to boot. The main actress, Jeanna Fine, really got his engines revving.

He could hardly wait to get one of the boosted DVD players from Christopher and Brandon. It was part of the deal; he gave them the info they desired, they offered him three thousand dollars and a brand-new player. He'd been quick to take the deal.

Stephen momentarily wondered what had roused him from his near-slumber, until the thunderous crash of a hammering fist on his front door clued him in. He glanced up at the wall clock and balked at the audacity of whoever was outside. It was the middle of the fucking night! What kind of rude fuck even does that shit?

"Hold your fucking horses, I'm coming!" Stephen hollered.

He flung the door open with rage, preparing to give the riot act to whoever was bothering him at this hour ... until he saw who it was.

It was Rossario Lochiano, the head of the KC mob. With his three capos, Vito, Sal, and that crazy bastard Paulie.

Stephen silently gulped in fear. It didn't take a rocket scientist to understand why they were here; it was over the stolen truck, and probably the driver. He decided he'd just play dumb and get these goombahs the fuck out of here so he could jack off to his favorite scene in *Edward Penishands* and call it a night.

"Mr. Lochiano! How is it going? What do I owe the pleasure of your company tonight?"

Rossario sauntered into the modest ranch home and surveyed his surroundings quickly and efficiently. You never knew when some fucker would try and whack you for a power play these days. That's why he always brought along his most trusted associates, and they all came heavy wherever they went.

Paulie glared at Stephen until the young man nervously tittered and looked away sheepishly. They followed their boss into the house like they owned the place, causing Stephen to backpedal.

"Uh ... how can I help you gentleman?" Stephen rasped.

"Don't play stupid, you fuck; you know exactly why we're here!" Paulie said.

"Yeah, let's skip the BS," Vito added. "Tell us what we need to know, and maybe we will go easy on your ass," Vito threatened.

Sal said nothing but kept his exposed pistol in plain sight.

It was obvious to Stephen why they were here, but he was unsure why they even cared about the heist. It wasn't their business, and they weren't being paid protection money from Comet Trucking, so what gives?

He was about to ask when Paulie barreled into his midsection, forcing him against the wall with a booming crash, causing the clock to tumble to the floor and break into fragments. The wise guy fixed him with smoldering, hate-filled eyes. Paulie's hair was slicked back and jet-black, except for the silver wingtips on each side of his head. His tailored suit was impeccable. His rough, calloused hands slammed into Stephen's chest, pinning him to the wall.

"The jig is up, you obdurate fuck … tell us what happened to the kid!"

"Kid? What are you talking about, Pau–   "

The punch was abrupt and brutal, the cartilage in the bridge of Stephen's nose immediately shattered. A sheet of blood fauceted down his astonished, wincing mug.

"Cut the shit, asshole, and tell us what we want to know, because that's the best this is going to get for you!" Paulie spat.

Rossario walked up to Stephen, looking him earnestly in his watering eyes.

"Look, we know you sold out that truck to get boosted," Rossario said. "I don't care about that aspect. What I do care about is the driver. Justin Fuller. Where is he? He's my little girl's fiancé, and she is worried about him. For your sake, he better be in tip-top shape."

His crumpled, flattened, nose now sat askew on his bloody, battered face. It dawned on Stephen the amount of shit he was in. Of all the people to be driving that truck why did it have to be someone affiliated with the *goddamned* mob?

He couldn't tell them the plan was to kill the driver; he had to figure out a way to stall, and possibly escape their clutches before they whacked him. He hadn't even received his cut from the fucking heist yet!

"Look fellas, all I know is, truck was robbed, I don't know shit about no murder– "

"Murder?" Sal questioned.

The temperature of the room became frigid.

"Who said anything about a murder?" asked Vito, with a soft, dangerous calm.

"You know you fucked up, right?" Paulie snarled. "You just narc'd out the whole deal. I suggest you give us the info on your cohorts, and don't make us ask twice!"

Stephen was flabbergasted that things had gone from shit to *deep* shit so spectacularly and quickly. His brain was going a million miles per second as he tried to spin some kind of believable yarn. A slap rocked his head violently to the side and expelled him from his deep thoughts.

He tried to say something, but before he could, Paulie drove a haymaker to his solar plexus, knocking the wind right out of him. He collapsed, gripping his midsection as he struggled to breathe.

Paulie stood above him, wearing a gleeful grin. He had been a powerful boxer in his prime, and he relished every opportunity he got to put his pugilist skills to good use. Violently grabbing Stephen by the throat, he hauled him up to his feet and lodged an elbow into his windpipe with crushing force.

Rossario surveyed as impassively as if watching a film. "It's late," he said, "and I want answers. Where is Justin?

What did you worthless jackals do to him? Answer me now, or so help me God, you'll be sorry."

Difficult though it was to speak, with his flattened blood-clogged nose and Paulie's elbow digging into his larynx, Stephen croaked out, "I'm telling you straight, I wasn't there, I don't kno–"

The report from the forty-five was almost as loud as Stephen's wails. The slug demolished his kneecap, obliterating the joint and damaging part of the femur. His leg looked like an M-80 had detonated inside of his flesh. The meat had been shredded into gory ribbons of chunky, pulpy, gristle.

Stephen plummeted to the floor again, holding the destroyed body part tightly with both hands and trying to apply pressure to the bleeding fissure.

"Oh, did that break your concentration?" Paulie said. "Please continue. You were about to lie to our faces, I believe."

The others regarded the mess calmly. It was something they had all grown accustomed to in their line of work.

Rossario knelt so he could look at Stephen eye to eye.

"Tell us what we want to know. Tell us where we can find him. It's over. Just spill the beans and make it easy on yourself."

"Look, it wasn't my fault! I didn't tell them to kill the driver; they came up with that part of the plan on their own!" Stephen whimpered.

Rossario shook his head. "That's neither here nor there. You got the ball rolling on this whole situation. You might not have intended bloodshed, but it's just as much your fault as theirs, make no mistake about it. Now, tell us what we need to know. Or keep being a pain in the ass, and we'll go visit your dear old mother. I'll have Paulie here hack her up into tiny pieces and feed them to my dogs."

"It would be my pleasure to off that old, worthless cunt, boss!" Paulie said, grinning.

Stephen croaked in agony and began to blubber. "Okay, okay, okay! My address book ... Brandon Ricci and Christopher Rossi ... those are the guys. They were gonna do the job at the intersection of Cunningham and Miller."

"See? That wasn't so hard, was it?" Rossario asked.

When the Don stood up, he looked at Paulie and gave him a subtle nod.

Paulie instantly shoved Stephen down onto his back and applied the heel of his perfectly shined Italian shoe to his throat. Stephen fought weakly, but he couldn't breathe. He heard and felt a *crunch*. He thought it was his Adam's apple. Everything turned hazy as Paulie added even more torque to his esophagus.

Blood sprayed from Stephen's grimacing mouth as his body desperately tried to breathe to no avail. Grotesque retching, gurgling sounds eked their way out of him as the men, bemused, watched his waning moments.

Paulie put the final nail in the casket by stomping on Stephen's gasping, upturned face. Up and down, a pummeling, stomping assault, fracturing his cheekbones and splitting his lips. Stephen's right eye swelled shut, the flesh ballooning until barely a slit peeked through purplish, black skin.

***

By the time Paulie finished stomping, he'd created a grapefruit sized lump in the middle of Stephen's forehead. T he head itself was swollen to the size of a pumpkin. Blood oozed out from every facial orifice imaginable.

When Paulie stopped, gasping fiercely from the deadly workout he just performed, he used the dead man's shirt as a makeshift door mat to wipe the excess blood and body fluids from his expensive shoes   .

Rossario gave the corpse a cursory glance before turning his full attention back to his comrades. He held up the address book.

"Okay, let's go check out Cunningham and Miller Road, and see if they left any evidence. If that's a dud, we'll try this Brandon Ricci's place; it's closer than Rossi."

"Sounds good, boss," Sal agreed.

"I'll drive,' Vito said. "I know right where that intersection is." With that, the four men headed back outside to the Lincoln Town car.

Rossario prayed silently for Justin to be okay, for the sake of his baby girl. His gut once again told him otherwise. He tried his best to ignore its gnawing refuting for at least a little bit longer.

Chapter 3

The Body

Arriving at the desolate spot of road, they fanned out and began to search.

Rossario had a heavy heart while he rooted through the overgrown brush with a stout branch. He was ninety percent sure Justin was dead. What little hope he still held was strictly for his daughter's sake. He glanced over his shoulder and saw Vito, Sal, and Paulie also searching hard and heavy. It warmed his heart to have not only such great friends, but excellent captains as well.

His heart sank, however, when he felt the branch hit something that wasn't weeds and dirt. Without hesitation, Rossario knelt and unearthed Justin Fuller from a hasty, clumsy, shallow grave.

His head had been destroyed by a high-caliber pistol round, executioner style. The lowlife bastards had ensured that he wouldn't even be able to have an open casket funeral.

"Hey fellas, get over here!" Rossario called.

Sal, Vito, and Paulie came lumbering over. They winced at the grisly sight.

"Is that him? Your future son-in-law?" Paulie asked.

Rossario looked down at the split open visage. The bullet had really done a number on him. Besides cleaving his head apart when it exited his wrecked cranium, it had also left blackened burn marks on his cheek and the bridge of his nose.

An army of black ants were already making themselves at home. Their tiny, bloody tracks peppered Justin's face like crimson freckles.

He sighed. "Yeah, it's him. He could hardly imagine having to break the news to her. "Those fuckin' cretins didn't have to shoot him! They're gonna pay for this!"

All three capos nodded in silent agreement with Rossario's impassioned rant. Sal walked up and lightly touched his shoulder, causing him to involuntarily flinch.

"We'll get these mad dogs," Sal swore. "And we'll make them pay too!"

Rossario smiled, but it was a mean grin full of cruel intent.

"First things first," he said. "Let's load him up and get me home. I need to let Nancy know what happened. Then we can get the ball rolling on a funeral and see about getting these degenerate murdering cocksuckers outfitted in some cement shoes!"

"Now we're talking!" Paulie smacked a fist into his open palm.

As the others loaded Justin's body into the trunk, Rossario frowned, already dreading the talk with his daughter.

Nancy was a fragile girl; she had taken after her mother in that department. Prone to fits of hysteria, she'd been a cutter in her youth, leaving her skin adorned with a legion of pale, ugly scars. She wore frumpy, oversized hoodies and sweatpants to hide her secret shame.

Rossario's wife, Julie, had battled her whole life with depression and ultimately took her own life. One day, when Rossario and Nancy had gone to the carnival, they'd arrived home to find Julie hanging by a noose in the closet.

He always feared the same fate would befall his daughter, but she had been the picture of mental health for over three years. He hoped she would hold it together now, and if she couldn't, he would get her the help she needed. He wasn't going to lose her too.

***

At first, she wouldn't even listen.

Then, she insisted on seeing the body. Rossario initially refused, but she was adamant and started flinging herself into the walls hard enough to send paintings crashing to the floor.

He had grabbed her by the shoulders and forcefully shook her as hard as he could, yelling for her to *snap out of it*. Once she had promised to try and calm down, he led her outside to the car and stood by the trunk, keys in hand.

"Are you sure, honey?"

"I'm sure. I just want to see him again, one last time."

"It's not pretty, I'm afraid."

"Death rarely is, Daddy."

Rossario nodded at her acute observation and drove the key home into the locking mechanism. When it clicked, he slowly raised the trunk lid, the darkened area illuminated by the interior light.

Watching his daughter's face crumble in absolute misery hurt his heart more than he ever could have imagined. He held her the best he could as she at first raged against his chest and then wept, desperately doing all he could to try and alleviate her pain. But in the end, he was a poor substitute for her massive malaise.

Back inside, he had gotten her a stiff drink of whiskey. She downed it in one gulp, like they used to do in the movies. It momentarily shocked Rossario, but the staunch drink did its job and numbed her to the point where she wasn't screaming like a banshee or trying to injure herself any longer. She gave her father a wan smile and gingerly placed a kiss on his wrinkled forehead. He looked at her with astonished eyes. He thought she for sure would have to be sedated to calm down to this level.

"I love you, Daddy," Nancy slurred. "I'm going to bed, I feel very, very tired all of a sudden."

"That sounds like a good idea, pumpkin. Do you need me to do anything for you?"

"Nope. I just need to sleep … *perchance to dream.*"

"Well okay then. Goodnight. I'll check on you in a little while, okay?"

"Sure thing."

With that, she slowly plodded up the vast staircase to her room. Rossario stared after her for a long time, even when he was no longer able to see her lilting form.

The last thing he heard before he went to his own quarters was Nancy's bedroom door closing behind her.

***

Rossario awoke in a cold sweat, gasping for air and utterly terrified.

He quickly surveyed his immediate surroundings and confirmed that he was in his own bed. The red LEDs on the alarm clock showed 4:45 AM.

A dream. An awful dream.

In it, when he had gone to remove the body of Justin from the trunk, he was shocked to find his daughter in there with him. Eating his flesh, tearing great handfuls of viscera out of his torso, slurping his ruptured brains out of the cavernous hole in his skull like linguini noodles. She'd noticed Rossario staring at her in flabbergasted horror, and smiled at him, flecks of meat and brain matter adorning her grisly, blood-speckled face.

"I'm eating for two now, Daddy!"

She then magically procured a straight razor and cut her belly open, reaching inside of her hemorrhaging guts and extracting a clearly dead infant. A boy. With the exact bullet wound as his father. His tiny, deflated head hung limply to the side.

"Like father, like son!" Nancy screeched.

That was all he could remember of the sickening nightmare. He sat upright and tried to get his trembling under control.

Once he felt like he wouldn't keel over as soon as he got out of bed, he went to Nancy's room, taking the staircase two steps at a time. When he got to her door, he suddenly became very afraid to open it. A thousand ghoulish thoughts raped his fragile mind as he stood there, his hands shaking like a palsied old man's as they gripped the ornate handle.

With a massive deep breath, he opened the door and turned on the lights.

"No … No! No! No! NoNoNoNoNoNONONO!" he screamed.

His beautiful girl was slumped in her bed, a straight razor still clasped in her tight grip. She had cut her wrists vertically to insure there would be less chance to save her if Rossario was lucky enough to discover her mid-cutting. Nancy's sheets had been doused, maroon from the inundation of her massive blood loss.

He grabbed his dead daughter and held her stiff form against his shuddering body. He briefly rubbed her belly and thought about the dead grandchild inside. This would have been his only chance to be a grandfather.

The weapon she had used to end her young life fell from her stiff hand. It was Hello Kitty branded. He recognized it immediately. When Nancy had first gotten into cutting, she had purchased a custom blade with the anime cat plastered all over it. She'd been trying to emulate a Japanese cutter she had befriended on Twitter, named Sadako.

Rossario had found it and disposed of it at one of his legitimate businesses, Soprano Trash Service. But apparently, she had purchased another of the fucking deadly things! He held her cold corpse against him as he cradled her and cried like he had never cried before. A parent should never have to deal with the death of a child. He felt like his heart had been excavated out of his chest with a dull knife.

He delicately kissed her cold, blue lips and gently brushed her hair to the side before placing her back into her bed and covering her with her bloodstained comforter.

When he rose to his feet his knees popped in protest, but he ignored them. He went into the front room and called

Paulie.

"Hey, I need you to round up those thieving fucks. And some of each of their family members."

"Not a problem boss! Want me, Sal, and Vito to plug 'em?"

"No. I want them to suffer more than they could have ever imagined possible. I want their families to suffer too! Unfathomable agony, to be precise!"

"What did you have in mind? We could always feed them to the pit bulls over at Carlo's --"

"No, that's too kind for them … Deliver everyone to Hardware Tony's."

The phone was dead silent on the other end. Then Rossario heard Paulie audibly gulp.

"Damn boss, you must really be in a vendetta kind of mood. Sending people to Hardware Tony's is like sending 'em to Hell … but ten times fucking worse! Are you fuckin' sure about this?"

"I've never been surer of anything in my life. Get it done."

Chapter 4

Flies In the Web, Part 1

Paulie chose Brandon's family first, targeting his son, AJ. He had some associates wait outside the boy's elementary school. They effortlessly abducted him the minute he was off the property. Two low level thugs in ski masks ran up and slammed the boy into a brick wall, knocking him out. They then loaded him into a nondescript white van and tore off down the road.

The next step was when Paulie, Sal, and Vito went to Brandon's house later that night, where his unsuspecting wife Charmaine let them in.

Paulie took in the meek surroundings of the Ricci home. *What a shit box,* he thought to himself. "You guys never heard of a broom around here?"

His face may have looked cheerful, but Paulie's eyes were predatory.

Charmaine's shamed eyes dropped to the floor like she was searching for something she had lost down there.

Just then, Brandon came in through the back door. "Nah babe, the Melfi's haven't seen AJ all day," he said, sounding worried. "Nobody's seen hide nor hair of him since school. I'll make a few ca–"

Brandon abruptly stopped speaking when he saw the three men in his living room. One look at his wife's nervous face was all he needed to know that these guys weren't concerned neighbors.

"What's going on?" Brandon croaked. "Who are you people? What the hell are you doing here?"

"Hey, is that any way to talk to the fellas who found your boy?" Paulie replied.

Charmaine's head shot up and the cloud of miasma surrounding her dissipated almost at once. "You found our boy? You found AJ?"

"Sure did. Just like your dear hubby *found* that truckload of DVD players... right, Brandon?" Paulie goaded.

Brandon went from feeling worried to feeling sick and absolutely terrified. "Look, if this is about that, I'll return everything immediately. We just want our son back, okay?"

"It's a little late for that, Brandon. We're way beyond you doing the right fucking thing now. Your little heist got a driver killed, remember?"

Charmaine gasped and looked at Brandon, but Paulie went on before she could say a word.

"And guess what, sport? That driver? He was important to somebody. Somebody you *don't* want to fuck with. Does the name Rossario Lochiano ring a bell?"

Brandon gulped in horror at the mention of the infamous mob boss. "We never meant to cross Mr. Lochiano. You got to believe me!"

Paulie's fist shot out like a piston and slugged Charmaine right in the face. Her head snapped back, and she fell to the floor, bleeding, too shocked to cry out.

Brandon stared at her, stunned.

"Oh, I'm sorry, did I break your concentration?" Paulie said, sneering. "I guess it's only fair, since I broke this cooze's nose, *right?*"

Before Brandon could reply, the phlegmy, aged voice of his father piped up from his bedroom.

"What's going on out there? Some of us need our rest, goddammit!"

"It's okay, Dad," Brandon managed to call. "It's fine!"

Paulie chuckled. "Might as well get his ancient ass out here too. Unless you want us to mail your brat home in pieces."

"He's got emphysema," Brandon protested. "He can barely move!"

"Then you better have your cunt of a missus go get him, or I'm going to turn this place into the fuckin' *Wild Bunch* in about two fucking seconds!" Paulie looked lethal, on the verge of frenzy. Sal and Vito also looked ominous behind him, but they said nothing. They just glared blackly.

Charmaine scrambled up and headed for the hall. "Be right there, Dad!" Thanks to her busted nose, her voice had taken on a clogged, whistling quality.

"Cunt sounds like a fucking boiling tea kettle," Paulie mused.

"Can we talk about this?" Brandon asked.

"Nothing to talk about. I'm just going to collect your family and take you on a little road trip. Reunite you with your boy."

Charmaine returned, pushing Brandon's father, Furio, in a wheelchair. Paulie thought he looked like a skeleton dipped in a jaundiced colored wax.

Hardly worth bringing along, but the boss said everyone, Paulie told himself.

"What is all this?! What are you hooligans doing in our house? Get out of here before I call the authorities!" Furio fumed.

Paulie smiled in a sardonic manner. The old cocksucker had sand, had to give him that. But they didn't need some emaciated old codger giving them a hard time.

With the butt of his gun, he gave the geriatric geezer a good crack against the temple, knocking him out and further horrifying Brandon and Charmaine in the process.

"Alright," he said to Sal and Vito. "Let's load these losers up and get the show on the fucking road; we don't have all goddamned night."

Chapter 5

Flies In the Web, Part 2

After dropping off the Ricci family, they made for the Rossi home. The drive passed mostly in silence; the three men lost in their own thoughts.

It wasn't like they weren't used to death and violence. Whacking people was almost an everyday occurrence, damn near part of the job description. But this time, this was an altogether different kind of animal. This involved Hardware Tony, a bona fide American psycho.

Paulie didn't mind the prospect, but Sal and Vito weren't so sure. They'd heard plenty of stories about Hardware Tony. He was almost an urban legend. Parents would tell their kids to be good, or else Hardware Tony would toss them into a woodchipper.

Some people even said that Rossario had sent Louie Ferrigno to the murdering lunatic a few years back. Reportedly, Ferrigno had raped one of Nancy's teen friends and cut her face up with a knife, deforming the poor girl beyond belief. So, Rossario had rounded up that pedophile fuck and sent his ass to Hardware Tony's.

Sal and Vito had only heard stories of the specifics, like what he did to Lou's cock, but Paulie had seen *pictures*. He'd tried to explain, but it was like speaking another language.

"You ever heard of *sounding*?" Paulie had asked.

"You mean, like, listening or some shit?" Sal responded.

"Or like sounding someone out?" Vito asked.

"Geez you two need to get out more, surf the internet or somethin'! It's this freaky sexual kink where you stick a metal rod up your urethra."

"Your what?" cried Sal.

"Your peehole," Vito answered helpfully.

"I know that, just ..."

"Anyway," Paulie went on, irritated, "sounding tubes are meant to be used medically, but some sickos get off on it, I guess because the tube can reach sensitive parts way up inside a guy's dick that, if stimulated, make him cum super hard."

"Jesus wept! Can't people just fuck a wet cunt anymore?" Sal wondered aloud.

"Had a nephew I walked in on in the bathroom once, and he had the handle of a hairbrush jammed up his ass while he was beating his meat!" Vito said.

"What'd you do?" Sal asked.

"I did a complete one-eighty and got the fuck out of there. I didn't even want to know why."

"Well, that's truly some fascinating shit and all, but can I please finish my fucking story?" Paulie seethed.

"Sure, thing Paulie, carry on!" Vito said.

"Okay, so, like I was saying, *sounding* is normally a sex thing, but not the way Hardware Tony did it. He shoved a twenty-two-inch screwdriver up Louie's tube steak and didn't stop until the handle was clear to his dick slit."

Sal and Vito made helpless sounds of disgust.

"Then," Paulie went on, warming to and relishing his tale, "that *fottuto pazzo figlio di puttana* started jackhammering that tool up and down until blood was fountaining out of Louie's dick hole like crimson cum! When he extracted that giant fucking screwdriver, all sorts of gore came with it, like a shish kabob from Hell!"

"That's fucking morbid!" Sal cried.

"My dick hurts just thinking about it!" Vito winced.

And now, a couple bonehead crooks, and their entire families, were going to get the Hardware Tony treatment.

First, though, they had to round up the other dimwit and his family. For the rest of the ride, they each contemplated how this next scenario might go. Would it be a cakewalk, like at Brandon's? Or would somebody try to kick up dust with some cowboy-type shit, and they'd need to regulate them? Only time would tell, they all supposed.

When they arrived, they were more prepared than ever. Having already performed the task once, they were confident it would go smoothly.

They gathered on the porch of the two-story house. From within, they could hear a television, and see into the entryway through a window in the front door, stairs leading up to the second floor. Paulie rang the doorbell.

"Who could be here at this hour?" a man grouchily complained.

"Shh, my program is on!" said an older woman.

Then, from upstairs ...

"I'll get it!" a girlish voice chirped. "I know how hard it is for you old people to get out of your recliners!"

... and a buxom teenager bounded down the steps, her ample breasts bouncing as only young titties can.

"Mama Mia!" Paulie murmured.

The door opened and the radiant teen girl smiled at them with a dazzling, perfect set of teeth. Her skin was a bronze tan, not a blemish to be seen. Her beautiful, brown hair had a natural curl.

She looked like the happiest girl in the world.

"Hi! Can I help you?" she asked.

Paulie gave the teen his most harmless and reassuring grin. "Hey sweetheart, my name is Paulie. These two are Sal and Vito. And yes, you absolutely can help us. Let me show you how."

In a flash, he had her in a chokehold, one arm hooked around her throat, the other holding her curvaceous young body snug against his, her tight rump pressed to his growing erection.

"Meadow?" called the man. "Who is it?"

"Okay, princess," Paulie hissed in her ear. "Here's how things are going to go. We're gonna march in there and pay a visit to your piece of shit pops. You get too frisky, and I'll carve up that pretty face until the horniest loser in the world won't even look at you. Got it?"

She bobbed her head hastily, like her life depended on it. Tears funneled down her reddened cheeks.

Paulie roughly escorted her toward the family room, Vito and Sal on his heels, closing the door behind them.

"Meadow?" the man called again.

He, bowl of popcorn in his lap, could only be Christopher. The other two were women, one close to Christopher's own age, the older one probably somebody's mother, looking indignant at this interference with her program.

"What the fuck?" Christopher blurted as Paulie entered

with Meadow held before him.

Both women froze, gaping, wide-eyed and astonished.

"Time to pay the piper, you degenerate, thieving asshole," Paulie said.

Sal and Vito fanned out to cover the room, guns drawn, as the old woman bestirred herself.

"Christopher, what's going on?" she yammered. "Who are these hooligans?"

"Can it, bitch," Paulie told her. "Or the princess here will be sorry!"

Meadow shivered like a leaf, and the old woman shut her trap. The other woman held her hands up pleadingly at Paulie.

"Please, mister, my daughter hasn't done anything. Just let her go, okay? Whatever you've got against Chris—"

"Hey, lady, I got nothing against him personally. But my boss, he sure does. Rossario Lochiano, maybe you heard of him?"

Their almost comic expressions said that, yes, they had.

"If you're talking about that big rig," Christopher said, talking fast, sweating, "Comet Trucking's not affiliated with Lochiano in any way… I checked, dammit!"

"Okay, smart guy … but did you think to check if the driver you killed was associated with him?"

Christopher wormed uneasily in his chair.

"Christopher, what is he talking about?" the old woman demanded. "What big rig? What driver? What does he mean, killed?"

"Carmella!" cried the other woman, her gaze still on her daughter and Paulie. "Be quiet, for God's sake!"

"Don't you get snippy with me, Adriana, I have a right to ask– "

Paulie looked at Christopher. "You shut them up, or we will," he said. "Permanently."

"Both of you, knock it off!" he shouted. "Let me handle this!"

They both scowled at him like rage incarnate. The room was thick with a smog of contempt for Christopher; no matter how much they loved him, he had brought this trouble to their door. Killing someone connected to the mob boss of Kansas City? And now these thugs were in their home. Meadow in their dangerous grip, fear plastered all over her gorgeous face.

Paulie's eyes gleamed in malevolent mirth as he watched the terror physically eat away at the women away like a scrumptious meal. If he loved anything more than himself, it was seeing his victims suffer copious amounts of misery.

Some of that must have shown on his face, because, orders to shut up aside, Adriana began to cry and beg him not to hurt her baby.

"What do you want us to do? Just tell us and we'll do it, no questions asked, just please don't hurt my baby!" Adriana cried.

"You mean, hurt her like… *this?*" Paulie tightened the chokehold, cutting off all air supply to Meadow's windpipe.

She struggled, clawing at his arm, already turning purple with her tongue hanging out of her mouth like a spent phallus.

"PLEASE STOP!!" Adriana wailed. As she made to lunge

from her seat, Sal leveled his gun at her, and she subsided.

Christopher, meanwhile, rose to confront Paulie, upending his popcorn bowl, only to be conked on the head with the butt of Vito's Glock 21. He dropped into a stupor, bleeding from a lacerated scalp wound.

Carmella mewled softly and held herself by the shoulders, her gnarled, arthritic fingers gripping the fabric of her sweater desperately as she nervously rocked back and forth in distress.

Satisfied that Christopher was out of commission, Paulie relinquished Meadow's swollen, reddened neck, allowing her to suck lifesaving air into her burning lungs.

"Alright, listen up," he said. "We are going to go for a ride to a very special place. Think of it as a funhouse, haunted house type of spot, I suppose. The guy who runs it is a real character too!" He felt like he was glowing with pungent pleasure, basking in their fear.

"If we go with you, do you promise not to hurt us?" Adriana queried.

"I won't hurt a single hair on any of your pretty little heads. Scout's honor!" He even held up his right hand while making the Boy Scouts gesture.

If a genuinely vile smile stretched across his face that in no way put the women's minds at ease, well, what could they do? They were definitely between a rock and a hard place. They were at the mercy of these horrendous hoodlums and there wasn't a *damn thing they could do about it.*

Utterly defeated, Adriana bowed her head. "We surrender, just lead the way so we can get this nightmare over with."

"Sal, Vito, would you mind escorting the ladies? That

knocked out cocksucker, you can toss into the trunk after you put some zip ties around his dick beaters. I'll take care of the little princess myself."

And just like that, the Rossi family was being led to their doom, with hardly any resistance whatsoever, just as the Ricci's had earlier that evening.

Chapter 6

The Devil's Playground

Once Adriana, Meadow, and Carmella sat their rumps within the confines of the expansive Lincoln Town car, Paulie required them each to ingest a dubious looking pill. Adriana thought they might be Rohypnol, or *roofies* as they were more commonly known.

It didn't take long before the drugs took hold and sent them into a near catatonic state. A feeling of fogginess smacked all three Rossi ladies like a Mack truck. Then a wave of sedation encapsulated them, followed by an immense feeling of paralysis and disorientation, before they finally passed out in the back seat.

After going for what felt like miles on the highway, the Lincoln veered off onto a gravel road like one would find out in the boondocks. It went on for what felt like forever, heading further into more dense woodlands. Eventually, it arrived at what appeared to be a warehouse in the middle of nowhere, which seemed nefarious in and of itself.

Sal pulled up to the loading area and honked twice. A second later, the large, overhead door rose with a grinding, whirring sound that reverberated throughout the dense foliage. The big Lincoln drove in, and the oversized door slowly droned back down and locked into place.

As Paulie got out of the vehicle, a beefy man strode into the loading area wearing a bloody butcher's apron. A contorted grin stretched the entire length of his chubby, stubbled face. Hardware Tony might have had a fat gut and chipmunk cheeks, but under his bulky exterior was a large surplus of muscle. Paulie knew from experience how strong Hardware Tony was. He had even been on *The World's Strongest Man* in the late eighties, coming in fifth place.

Tony strode up to Paulie and gripped his hand crushingly firm with his massive meat hook. "Hey Paulie, long time no see! What have you been doing with yourself? You still been fucking your mom at night?"

"Va Fangool!" Paulie retorted.

"Relax, pasian, I'm just breaking your balls!"

"In case you forgot, big man, I don't *like* my balls broken!"

"Why else do you think I do it, then?"

Paulie had to begrudgingly smile at the oversized man's banter. He hated to be teased, but sometimes you must give the devil his due.

Hardware Tony gazed into the big Lincoln at the drugged occupants passed out inside. He looked like a kid in a candy store, all but drooling in anticipation of the sweets.

"Four more, huh? A total of eight to play with? This is going to be spectacular! I'll use my coolest toys to teach these people a valuable lesson to not fuck with the Don! Who's the girl?"

"Meadow Rossi."

"Mm, Meadow. Just rolls off the tongue, doesn't it?" Tony leaned in and licked the incapacitated girl's swan-like neck. "How much damage do you think I could do to this little angel's face with a weed whacker?"

"Madone!" Paulie exclaimed.

"Or I could use needle nose pliers and flay her skin off one strip at a time," Hardware Tony suggested.

"It's your world. Do as you wish. Rossario just requests that they suffer till their very last breath."

"My specialty! You can relax on that request. Mr. Lochiano can, too!"

"I'll make sure and tell him that," Paulie said.

"Plus, I set up a feed for Mr. Lochiano, so he can watch the excitement from the comfort of his own home."

Tony handed Paulie a meticulously hand-written URL address on a business card from a place called *Pierce & Pierce*. Paulie noticed that it was printed on bone colored paper with *Silian Rail* typeface. He shoved it into his overstuffed wallet.

"I'll make sure and give it to him, although he's all thumbs with technology. Now, let's get these cocksuckers out of the car so you can work your magic."

"Sounds magnificent. I'll get tons of pictures as well! Help me bring all this delectable meat to the various stations. I can promise an interesting and painful demise for them all!"

As they worked, unloading the bodies and placing them as per Tony's instructions, Paulie looked at the numerous tools on display and winced. Hardware Tony was a certified nutjob to be sure, but the paisan had panache!

Sociopath though he was, he still found himself wondering if the punishment fit the crime for everyone. Christopher and Brandon deserved it, of course, but the women? The kids?

It was debatable, he supposed. At the end of the day, though, he really had no fucks to give. He wouldn't piss on their corpses if they were on fire.

"Fuck with the bull and you get the horns," Paulie said.

"The boss is the bull, and I am the horns!" Hardware Tony added, cackling diabolically.

***

Tough guys though they were, once everything was set up, Paulie, Sal, and Vito bade farewell and departed, leaving Tony to his own devices.

Fine by him. He didn't mind an audience, but he didn't require one either.

He slowly walked around the stations, affectionately inspecting his newly captive victims. Each was secured to a chair, manacled at the wrists and ankles, unconscious, bound, and stark naked.

It wasn't a sexual thing; Tony was, in fact, a sanguinarian, or blood fetishist. Male or female genitals did nothing to rev his libido. The only thrill Hardware Tony was able to achieve was from his immense bloodlust. He'd only had the goombahs strip them down to their birthday suits to make his task easier.

But which family to tear asunder first? Tony couldn't pick, so he decided to flip a coin.

"The Rossi's it is!" Tony declared.

But who to start with? Hardware Tony was a fan of Meadow, but he wanted to hold off on her. She was more of a "main course" type, in his mind's eye. He wanted to build up the carnage so he could properly disfigure this goddess as she deserved. Christopher, per the Don's explicit orders, had to be butchered last. No way around that one, unfortunately.

That left the old woman or Meadow's mom. Tony settled on the old woman. She would be the opening act for his slaughter special.

Looking her over, he could see a ghost of the beauty she must have been, buried just under the surface like something illusory. But she had let herself go; too many years of heavy drinking had zapped her of any attractiveness and left a shriveled up old crone in its place. Her body was adorned with liver spots, and more skin tags than Tony thought was humanly possible.

He wondered when the last time she had even fucked someone was. Her pubic hair was a bristly gray thatch, like a huge mass of Daddy-Long-Leg spiders between her legs. Her pancake tits hung flatly against her chest, with areolas of a dark brown pigment that caused Tony's stomach to lurch in protest, nipples like crooked, protruding pinkie fingers. They even had a few spindly hairs sprouting out of them, for God's sake.

Maybe he was doing a kindness in eradicating this brittle old cunt's life.

But, how to go about it?

Then, in the way all good art is created, a eureka moment struck him with a vibrant mental picture. He loved the idea and was eager to get the show on the road.

Chapter 7

Meat Hook Sodomy

Cannibal Corpse, one of Tony's favorite bands, blared from the monolithic stereo. He loved their morbid cover art as well as their disgusting lyrics, and liked to think he brought their music to life when he used it for inspiration.

Some death metal bands relished in horror movie type imagery, but not Cannibal Corpse. Tony imagined that a real killer might write lyrics and songs like these. With titles like "Hammer Smashed Face," "Addicted to Vaginal Skin," and "Fucked with A Knife, just to name a few, you knew you were dealing with a band that liked to be controversial and push boundaries. All those songs were great, but Tony was going with his absolute favorite Corpse song.

Entitled "Meat Hook Sodomy," it was the lead track off their second album, *Butchered at Birth,* a true death metal classic in Tony's eyes.

Tony had moved the old woman -- Carmella, according to Paulie -- into an archaic gynecological chair he'd purchased years ago. The stirrups had her legs parted as far as they would go; Tony thought he heard her pelvic bone pop in protest. She appeared to be rousing, due to her body's painful placement. Tony wanted to make sure she was fully awake to enjoy the upcoming onslaught of agony, so he grabbed some smelling salts.

He always loved watching the concoction do its thing. The

way it worked was brilliant in its simplicity. Smelling salts were chemical compounds used as stimulants to restore consciousness after fainting. They worked by releasing ammonia gas that irritated the nasal and lung membranes when sniffed, thus causing a person to inhale more oxygen and breathe faster, which awakened and revived them. Weightlifters oftentimes used smelling salts for the adrenaline rush, to lift more weight than normal.

He also loved watching his victims emerge from their slumbers and realize they were in a world of shit.

Hovering the smelling salts under Carmella's nostrils, he waited as she inhaled the noxious mixture. Then her eyes snapped open like a trap, and she looked around the room in a fog of cluelessness.

"W-w-w-what's going on?" she stammered.

"What's going on is, to quote the *Bhagavad Gita: Now I am become death, the destroyer of worlds.*"

***

Carmella peered dubiously at him. She still felt groggy and out of the loop, and here was this giant beast of a man talking in tongues and quoting some gibberish to her. As awareness returned, spurred by the discomfort of her position, she realized she was nude and restrained in a gynecological chair. Her pelvic region screamed in agony.

She wanted to scream herself, wanted to scream her lungs out, summon help, raise hell, but the best she could do was an unsteady, "Why?"

"It's the price you must pay for birthing a degenerate son. If you had kept that squalid snatch closed, you wouldn't be here now. But don't worry, I am going to make sure that pesky pussy of yours never gets you into trouble ever again."

Carmella tried to speak, but he put a finger to her lips and shushed her. He then procured a gleaming metal hook and brought it to her flinching face.

"Do you know what this is?" She shook her head, a welling of tears spilling from her eyes. She was scared to death; she didn't know what the item was called, but she knew it was going to be used to inflict pain on her.

"It's a meat hook. They use them to hang up cattle on a moving conveyor line in a slaughterhouse, for *processing*."

Her tears flowed faster and she blubbered a sob.

"Let me be blunt, Carmella. I am going to take this hook and sodomize your ass with it. I might also fuck your vagina with it as well. Hell, I might even jab it through your pathetic, pancake tits! The options are limitless!"

Carmella heard the words, but her reeling mind couldn't comprehend them. It was like she'd forgotten the English language and could only glean some vague sense of meaning.

"Shall we begin?" he asked.

Not pausing for a reply, he placed the sharp point of the hook at the entrance to her puckered sphincter. She bucked and raised her ass in the air, but there was nowhere to go, no way to hide from the sharp metal. He efficiently fed the tip into her asshole like he had done this countless times before. Her anus almost immediately began weeping blood as he continued to slide the cold, surgical grade steel into her reluctant rectum.

"PLEASE GOD HELP ME!" Carmella wailed, bucking against her restraints as the hook tunneled deeper and deeper into her, the blood proving to be a fantastic lubricant.

Tony produced another meat hook, brandishing it. "*This* is God, bitch!"

***

Tony pushed the tip of the second hook through Carmella's left breast. It made a pleasant popping sound as it burst through the elastic, veiny tissue. The bloodied tip erupted through the other side of her abused mammary gland, ejaculating blood onto her shriveled belly.

He worked the hook into her other breast, piercing through both of her sagging *dirtypillows*. She screeched and squealed like a belligerent hog. Once he had skewered both tits completely, he slotted the meat hook into a winch that hung above Carmella's head from a chain, and ratcheted a crank. The hook rose, pulling her impaled bosom with it, stretching to the point where her skin began to split from the pressure.

She screamed mindlessly as both breasts tore raggedly from her body, dripping chunks suspended above raw, weeping flesh.

Without a single word of warning, Tony seized a third meat hook, plunged the cold steel deep into her withered, hairy, cunt.

"YYYYYAAAAARRRRGGGGHHHH!" Camella shrieked.

It was music to his ears to hear her moan and gobble in exquisitely acute agony. Tony pushed the barbaric tool further up her joy trail. Crimson, ruby fluid poured out of her vagina like a burst water main.

As he furiously fucked her wounded womb with the hook, he gazed into her eyes, like a lover might. Carmella's eyes rolled around in her sockets drunkenly, her synapses howling in protest at her pain center for this all to *stop*.

But there was no way to call off this anguish. A madman was at the wheel, and he was intent on sending her careening into the median to burst into flames.

Tony was up to his forearm in her gooey, gory gash when the tip of the meat hook sliced through her pubis mons like a shark's fin in the ocean.

"IT'S KILLING MEEEEEEEE!!!!"

"That's the point, silly!" Tony chortled.

Carmella emitted her most ear-piercing wail yet as the hook ripped through her flesh with tenacious determination. Her eyes bulged grotesquely from her sockets. Her body was drenched in sweat from the massive endorphin dump her system had created to combat the unfathomable agony. Brownish blood and shit and a steady stream of chunky clots rained from the grisly cleaved-open fissure her lower body had become, both hooks lodged deep and still carving deeper.

Her howls of torment created a nice rigid erection in Tony's pants. Precum dribbled from the bulbous head of his cock.

Finally, a bevy of purple intestines trundled out of the wrecked cavity, plopping to the floor with a splat. Carmella's punctured pancreas barfed out a deluge of greenish bile, soaking her pubic hair in the loathsome liquid. She continued screaming, spraying a fine mist of crimson into the air as she began to succumb to her horrendous wounds. Her thrashing became less pronounced and more languid as her essence carpeted the floor.

Tony watched in fascination as Carmella's eyes took on a faraway look– the death look, as he liked to call it. He brusquely grabbed her cheeks and turned her pained face to meet his breezy one.

"Look at me. I want to see the light go out, Carmella."

She stared at him helplessly as her fluids dispersed from her ravaged sexual orifices and her withered, flattened breasts swayed gently from the barbed hook above her like a pendulum. Droplets of blood softly plopped onto her pallid face.

As she succumbed to her massive injuries, Tony lightly tugged at his straining member through his pants. He glanced up at the mortified breasts, transfixed by the beautiful hue of the yellow fatty tissue peeking through the mangled meat.

Only then did he turn his attention to the next woman, whom Paulie had said was Adriana, as she groggily began to come to from the effects of the roofie.

"On to round two, where the stakes get higher, and the body count continues!" Tony laughed.

Chapter 8

Jackhammer Facial Obliteration

Adriana awoke with a start from a terrible nightmare of someone screaming for their lives as a monster viciously tore them to shreds.

Then, scanning the strange room, her eyes fell upon Carmella's ruined and ripped form. Her entire groin had been turned into one massive orifice, its yawning chasm drooling various internal organs from its cavernous depths. Above, her disembodied breasts swung from a shimmering meat hook, swaying like a pair of fuzzy dice hanging from a car's rear view mirror.

The sight was the most traumatizing thing Adriana had ever seen in her life. An overwhelming anxiety overtook her as she uselessly wrenched at the shackles locking her solidly into place.

"Hello? Anybody?" she squeaked.

Almost as if by osmosis, a large man appeared, eating a slice of pepperoni pizza. He smiled blissfully when he saw Adriana awake and lucid.

"Welcome to the land of the living! And just in time for your part in this cavalcade of carnage. My name is Hardware Tony, by the way. Had to step out for a quick snack."

She tried to make sense of what the monolithic man was jabbering about, but her eyes were drawn back to Carmella, her cadaver sprawled in what looked to be an ancient gynecological chair.

"Let me apologize in advance for what's about to happen," Tony went on. "I'm just a guy doing his job. Now, I'll not be facetious and try to portray myself as a saint; *I love my work.* Consider me a gore connoisseur. Anybody could use a gun or a knife, but that's way too impersonal for me. Lazy, too! I like to put some thought into it … some, dare I say, panache! What I do is parallel to artistry. I am a sculptor of slaughter."

Adriana felt the vestiges of a panic attack begin to swell, her heart beating erratically in terror.

"Look, mister," she pleaded shrilly, "It was Christopher, okay? We didn't have anything to do with it. We didn't know. He's the one you want. I mean, what about 'eye for an eye' and all that wise guy shit?"

Tony chuckled as if finding it quite comical how quickly she threw her man under the bus. For a fleeting moment, she let herself hope she could still get out of this.

"Nice try," he said. "Sorry to disappoint you, but you are deemed guilty by association. You're all gonna pay for what Christopher and his buddy Brandon did. Per Rossario Lochiano himself. Now, listen up because I have something truly spectacular in mind for you!"

"Noooooooooooo!" Adriana moaned.

She turned her head away from the maniac, like that would somehow cause him to vanish.

It's just a bad dream, she thought. *I will count to ten and open my eyes and it will have just been a nightmare.*

But, when she opened her eyes, the big, beefy man was still standing in front of her, eating the last of the pizza crust.

"Yup, still here! Now quit being silly thinking this isn't reality! Pinch yourself and you'll see that it will hurt! It's all true, Adriana. The boogeyman is real ... and you found him!"

Adriana looked desperately around, seeing Meadow -- unconscious but apparently unhurt, thank God! -- as well as Christopher. "Well then, where's Brandon at? What about his people? Why are we the ones that must suffer?"

"The Ricci's? Oh, they're here, but in the next room. I needed to make sure I had space for all my innovative ruthlessness. That, and I don't want them to know what's in store for them. It's even soundproofed! No spoilers, right?"

"I'll do anything you want, but *please*, spare my daughter," Adriana begged. "I'll fuck you, suck you, whatever! Just let her go! She's only a kid! She's going to be a veterinarian!"

Tony gave another chuckle, and slowly shook his head.

"Thanks, but nah. Sex doesn't interest me. *Pain*, though? Pain is my foreplay and gore is my intercourse. Blood is my cum. Your little girl's up next, after you."

Adriana began to sob, but one look from Tony's blazing eyes caused her throat and tears to dry up instantly. She looked again around the harshly lit room, illuminated by high bay fluorescent fixtures with high output bulbs, garishly bathing the horrific scene. Every detail of Carmella's grisly corpse was lit perfectly, showing off the details of her hollowed-out sex cavity like the pictures in a science book. Adriana retched, throwing up a little bit in her mouth, and reluctantly faced Hardware Tony again.

He was beaming at her like a kindly benefactor.

"I really think what I have for you is something truly special," he said. "Something that hasn't been seen before! I am beyond ecstatic to give it a try!"

Adriana stared dumbstruck at the man as he jubilantly gloated over whatever horrible plans he had in mind. She found herself thankful that Meadow was still knocked out; at least she wouldn't have to watch her mother be killed right in front of her.

And then there was Christopher, shackled prone on a wooden table, with his head clamped in a large vise. Adriana wept harder, but not over him.

Hadn't her own mother told her, shortly before Adriana ran away from home at age fifteen, that her taste in bad boys would be the death of her one day? She had scoffed at her mother's veiled threat then, but now, that bitter pill had to be swallowed. She was going to die because she had picked a wannabe criminal as her man. Her bad decisions were going to be the end not only of her life, but of Meadow's as well, before Meadow's life was even beginning.

A loud CLAP shocked Adriana out of her grim thoughts. Hardware Tony had smacked his big hands together stridently to snap her back to attention.

The worst part of it was that the creepy bastard was still smiling at her!

"Earth to Adriana, come in Adriana!" Tony chortled. "Now, listen up!"

He hefted a large device, the kind she associated with highway repairmen breaking up concrete. Fear immediately began to inundate her brain.

"What we have here is a pneumatic jackhammer," he said, as if he was making a commercial. "In layman's terms, a pneumatic hammer works with compressed air, which fills the piston, pushing the hammer's head. The air comes from a separate machine called a compressor, which is connected to the handle of the hammer through a valve. Fun fact: its current design is still very similar to the first hydraulic hammers from the late 19th century. Pretty neat, huh?"

Adriana followed the hose with her eyes and saw that it was indeed connected to an air compressor. Tony flicked the machine on, bringing it to life. The air compressor made an ungodly racket as it powered up the jackhammer.

"This type of hammer can be paired with various accessories," he went on, raising his voice to be heard over the noise. "Such as, say, chisels or drills, to perform different jobs more efficiently. Today, we'll be using the chisel attachment."

Adriana continued weeping silently, lamenting her existence as her life began flashing in her mind.

"It should nicely pulverize your facial features into a pulpy viscera. To try and prolong your suffering, of course, I'll save your brain for last. Now, this may or may not work; you could die instantly. That's the thing, I have never tried this. But you know what the old timers say: nothing ventured, nothing gained!"

Tony brought the jackhammer's chisel up to Adriana's chin and placed the tip against it. The rough metal already felt like it was burrowing into her delicate flesh. He looked at her in a meaningful way, like a compassionate priest during a confessional.

"Do you have any last words?"

Adriana considered begging again for the life of herself and her daughter, but knew her entreaties would be falling on deaf ears. This man was a monster, plain and simple. He was doing a job he fully intended on completing, and Adriana knew it.

She decided to take a gamble. She prayed that he would rage out and kill her quickly. That was the best possible scenario; maybe he'd simply prolong her death even more to get back at her for running her mouth. He struck Adriana as a vengeful type, relishing the power that his torture factory provided him.

Fuck it, she thought; *go big or go home*.

"Yeah, I got some last words," she said. "Try a fucking breath mint! Smells like you've been eating shit all morning long. And another thing, you fat fucking incel: it's not women's fault your micro dick can't get hard; it's your burden, because you're a *goddamned fucking psychopath!*"

A funny thing happened. Her words had a profound effect on Tony. She could see it in his eyes. He visibly flinched from her verbal strike against his manhood. She finally had broken that chipper exterior he had been exuding and was able to glimpse the sensitive side of the man, even if it was only for a moment.

***

His mask only slipped an instant before it was back in place, and Tony smiled cruelly at the doomed woman as he turned the jackhammer on. The sound was deafening. The chisel began chewing through Adriana's chin as it slammed into flesh and bone. Puncture wounds and gashes spilled blood down her torso as the machine effectively spiderwebbed her jaw, and then shattered it into fragments, causing the lower half of her face to droop askew.

Adriana moaned and screeched as the jackhammer went at her teeth next. Like a bowler's strike, the chisel violently blasted them, leaving the jagged roots embedded in her gums while shards of enamel flew like confetti in a parade. In a matter of seconds, her pearly whites were demolished, broken teeth scattered all over the warehouse floor.

"Pwwese stahp!" Adriana bloodily mushmouthed, the words almost alien in their mingling of unfamiliarity with familiarity.

Tony, however, understood her garbled speech, and it pleased him.

"So much for that tough girl façade!" he chuckled.

He raised the jack hammer to her left cheek. A wide swath of tissue unzipped, showcasing the glistening muscle behind the hemorrhaging epidermis. The bones were pulverized under the chisel's pounding wrath. Her facial structure began to collapse like a sinkhole, the entire left side of her face sagging grotesquely and taking on a stroke-like appearance. Still, the jackhammer repeatedly slammed in and out, bursting capillaries and shredding sinews in its furious wake. Blood flew chaotically, splattering everything in the vicinity with sludgy, crimson droplets.

Tony then moved to her right cheek and repeated the process, detonating the other half of her face with the cruel precision of the chisel's striking force.

"AAAAARRRRRGGGGGHHHHH!" Came her garbled,

inhuman cry.

All that remained of her mouth was the upper mandible; everything below had been destroyed. Her toothless gums leaked blood from the holes; nerves and blood vessels dangled limply from their housing. Her tongue lolled like a hangman's noose on the gallows. Her eyes bulged wildly as her body was wracked with unknowable pain.

Tony stabbed the chisel into one of her peepers. It immediately burst, spraying viscous reddish yolk. Driving deeper, he began jackhammering her orbital bone into sections, careful not to push all the way through into the brain just yet. He extracted the apparatus with her pulverized eye remnants still attached to it. The viscera left a gooey, stringy, rope of gore, like an extra cheesy pizza pie fresh from the oven. He then penetrated her other eye and made quick work of it as well, the powerful tool obliterating it into soup.

Still, the woman lived, though her unrecognizable face shook animalistically, spraying blood and bone flecks and demolished chunks of chewed up flesh around in a chaotic fashion. Even though she no longer had a mouth she was still able to make guttural howls and bestial groans.

Tony set the jackhammer's gore caked chisel against her ruby soaked forehead and pressed the switch to life once again. The chisel hammered through thin skin and into the dense, gleaming, porcelain skull beneath, before cracking that hard exterior in its unforgiving wrath. Cracks splintered across the bone like a frozen lake with too much weight on the waning ice.

Finally, the skull could no longer endure the punishing blows. It broke apart, jagged pieces driven inward, jamming their sharp ends into Adriana's brain. Tony continued his evil onslaught, blasting away at her exposed, vulnerable gray matter and turned it into Swiss cheese. Shredded chunks of ground up pulp vomited out of the wreckage of Adriana's forehead as Tony finished turning her head into a stew of chunky gore.

He turned off the raucous machine, returning the room to silence, but for the wet plopping of blood droplets and liquefied brain tissue on the concrete below.

Tony could only admire his newest horrific handiwork. Adriana's head had taken on a deflated, flat look. From the neck up, she no longer looked human. It was as if a grenade had been stuffed into her mouth and detonated.

To him, it was beautiful, a true work of art.

Grinning to himself, he turned and set his sights on Christopher, by then beginning to stir from his concussed stupor. The sight of his head -- no doubt still throbbing from the blow that had lacerated his scalp and put him down for the count -- locked into the massive vise-clamp made Tony wriggle in pleasure, like a child on Christmas morning.

In a way, Christmas or not, he'd be opening another present very soon himself. He ambled towards the moaning man in anticipation.

This was going to be a good one…

Chapter 9

My Vice Is Your Head In A Vise

Struggling to consciousness, Christopher tried to raise his aching head, and found he couldn't move it at all. Something held it tight, pressed on both sides.

His first thought was that he was in the hospital, immobilized in one of those collars for head and neck injuries. But what view he had of the area above him was certainly no hospital. All he could tell was that he was in an expansive industrial-looking space illuminated by garish fluorescent lighting.

Feeling sore, scared, and flustered, Christopher called out into the eerie, obdurate silence.

"Hello? Is there anyone here? What the fuck is going on?"

"Oh, hey! You're awake, excellent! We can start now!"

The high, chirpy voice wasn't one he recognized, but to him it sounded like it belonged to an effeminate man, swishy and gay. That would *not* be someone he associated with. But the heavy-set, powerful footsteps coming in his direction did not match the image his mind had already conjured.

Then a broad, stubbled, giddy face loomed above him, exuding excitement and pure delight. Christopher knew he had seen the face from somewhere before. He desperately searched through the useless files of his brain until he located the memory.

Tommy DeMarco's office, maybe six years ago, and there'd been a picture on the wall with this fat fuck in it. He was someone of note, someone with a name, and his brain worked feverishly, synapses firing on all cylinders, to remember.

Then it came to him and made his blood freeze in his veins.

Hardware Tony. He was in fucking Hardware Tony's kill room!

Christopher had heard horror stories about the guy for years, but used to think he was just some kind of boogeyman the goombahs used to mention with bated breath to freak out the new blood.

But here he was, Hardware Tony in the flesh.

And here was Christopher, a bug trapped in a web, with a giant Black Widow hungrily staring him in the face.

"Oh, shit," he muttered feebly.

"Oh, shit, indeed, my friend. You are in what we in the business call a bind. Bumping off that driver, who just happened to be Rossario Lochiano's daughter's fiancé?" He tutted and shook his head reprovingly. "Then, his daughter went and offed herself, to boot! Needless to say, the big man's ire was raised. That is why your head is currently clamped into this nice, oversized vise right here."

Of everything Hardware Tony had just said, the part that most stood out was that his literal *head* was in a goddamned *vise*!

Christopher burst into a terrified cold sweat. The chilly, unforgiving, forged steel seemed to press even more firmly at the sides of his skull.

Suddenly, another thought struck him, and his horror intensified.

"Where's my family?"

"Well ..." Tony rocked on his heels, clearly enjoying himself. "Your mother and main squeeze are dead, and the girl is next in line after you to be butchered beyond belief. I took a keen liking to her, so I am saving her for later. The better to extend my jubilation with her dismantling." He leaned closer, his smile becoming conspiratorial. "The boss told me to kill *you* last, but I am making an executive decision. Besides, I thought it would hurt you more, knowing what was going to happen."

The way this lunatic looked like a redneck shit-kicker but talked like an academic's major was all too much for Christopher's scrambled brains. Despite being mere moments from an agonizing death, he focused only on one thing: Meadow.

His beautiful daughter, being entwined in this fuckery, and it was all his fault. His and Brandon's. They hadn't needed to kill that driver, but they did anyway, his death meaning nothing. But now, fate had turned its murderous sights on their innocent families, like their lives were equally inconsequential.

His mom ... Adriana ... and Meadow next?

Christopher was still deep in his frantic thoughts when he felt the vise begin to tighten around his head. His brain momentarily shut everything down but its pain center as the pressure increased.

"Woah, woah, woah! PLEASE STOP!!!" Christopher wailed.

"Sorry, buckaroo; no can do! You have a date with getting your skull crushed. I don't want to prolong your death, anyway, because I have some special plans for that gorgeous daughter of yours."

With that, Tony began cranking the handle of the vise like a man possessed.

***

Around and around the vise handle spun, the jaws clamping tighter to the sides of Christopher's straining face. His complexion bloomed into an angry, red hue, capillaries bursting like tiny explosions as Tony continued to twist the handle of the merciless vise.

His shrieks of anguish were only matched by the crackling sounds of overstressed facial bones in his distorting, compromised visage. Christopher howled.

"YYYYYAAAAARRRRGGGHHHH! MY FUCKING HEAD!"

"Now we're getting the proper reaction!" Tony chortled.

"JUST KILL ME!" Christopher croaked.

"All in due time. The vise isn't exactly known for efficiency and speed, after all!"

Corded veins arose in Christopher's forehead as the crushing power of the oversized vise made true headway in its destruction of his cranium. His skull began to crumple and cave in on itself from the immense compression it was enduring. One of his eyes protruded, as if seeking to eject itself from its eye socket. It made Tony think of a chicken's constricted asshole squeezing out an egg.

With another turn of the lever, a champagne-cork sound heralded Christopher's eyeball shooting into the air like a popgun projectile tethered by an optic nerve. It plopped back onto his puffing cheek as a deluge of gore began to pour out of his newly excommunicated socket like a thick, blood-laced pudding.

Tony continued to turn the crank, fracturing the screaming man's cheekbones and jaw, and dismantling his orbital bones. His other eye was pulped in its housing, cut into ribbons by slivers of bone. poking into it. Splintered bones also burst from his cheeks, making Christopher's accordioning face look like a grisly pin cushion. Blood, laden with clots and stringy tissue, erupted from his facial orifices like miniature geysers.

As his skull collapsed into itself, his brain matter had no option but to spurt out those avenues of escape as well, from his grisly eye sockets and ears, and even his grimacing mouth, in chunky torrents. His dying body gyrated like an epileptic, releasing a stream of rank, yellow urine and an immense porridge textured flood of shit.

The distinct, cloying odors of foul-smelling piss and human excrement wafted up to Tony's nostrils, causing even him to flinch instinctively. "Jeez, killing can be such unpleasant work sometimes. Blood is one thing; shit and piss, not so much."

A final turn of the crank, and the jaws finally met, the remnants of Christoper's face flatter than a messy red pancake between them.

Hardware Tony wiped his carnage-caked hands off on what clean parts he could find of the dead man's shirt and smiled happily at the now-headless body. He had always wanted to use the vise on someone and was pleased to have finally done so.

The evening thus far had gone swimmingly. All that was left of the Rossi family was the delectable Meadow. His plans for the girl were going to be slow and painful. Extremely painful, just the way he preferred it.

And he still had another room full of victims waiting in the wings! This was shaping up to be the best night of his life.

***

Meadow was still out; the drugs evidently having hit her innocent young system harder than they had her mother and grandmother.

Deciding on a different setup, Tony moved her nude, shivering body from the chair to the cold, concrete floor, reaffixing her restraints to ring bolts in the concrete. Then, grinning like a fiend, he fetched the items he planned on using for an appetizer on the young beauty.

A noticeable bulge grew in his pants as he regarded the captive girl. Seeing her finally start to stir, he thought he'd help her along, and figured urinating on her pristine face was just the way to do it.

A pint of putrid piss proved the perfect rude awakening. Meadow twisted her head to the side, violently spitting and hacking and coughing, having been nearly drowned.

"Oh my God, what --?" she sputtered.

"Wakey wakey, eggs and bakey!" Tony singsonged.

"Scooby Dooby Doo, we got some work to do now!"

She looked up at him in confusion that quickly turned to terror. A giant man was looming over her with his dick out, leering like a homicidal rapist about to rip her virginal vagina to shreds!

Although Tony's main plans had little to do with her snatch, he did plan on ripping her apart in other ways, with his signature style and panache.

"How about a little foreplay before we get down to the nitty gritty, Meadow my love?"

As she started thrashing and screaming and hollering for help, he held up his two items of choice: a canister of SABRE brand Frontiersman Bear Mace with the maximum strength allowed by the E.P.A. of 2% major capsaicinoids, and a Metabo brand pneumatic nail gun.

Chapter 10

Nail Gun Massacre With a Side of Bear Mace

Meadow stopped screaming and thrashing, just trembled like a lone leaf on a dying tree as she stared at Hardware Tony from her vulnerable spot on the frigid floor of the warehouse.

He saw her open her mouth, no doubt about to spout some formulation of words to try and talk her way out of this nightmare scenario, just like her mother had. Not needing to hear all that again, he let her have it full in the face with a thick, foaming jet of bear mace. Her head jerked back forcefully, smacking the back of her skull against the unyielding concrete. Her eyes involuntarily squeezed shut.

The pain must have been all-encompassing, like acid injected directly into her eyeballs. What had gone into her mouth caused her to gag and retch up mucus-like strands of bile and drool. She could barely breathe, her respiratory system under attack. the cloud of irritants lingering like an early morning fog. Where the mace hit her unblemished, supple skin, it immediately became reddened and damaged like a severe sunburn. Meadow yowled in torment as the chemical spray incapacitated her in misery.

"Well, I guess it hurts," Tony said smugly.

He was just about to put the can down when he got an even more mean-spirited idea, one too delicious not to indulge in.

Kneeling between Meadow's splayed, manacled legs, he regarded the delicate folds of flesh between them in utter disbelief.

This was the area that controlled most men's minds. This little hole, the root of all evil. He hated it because he didn't understand it. Even as a boy, when he and his friends snuck off with a few of their dads' *Hustler* magazines, he hadn't felt anything, except maybe disgust. The others all would get their minuscule erections and hoot and holler over the lewdness of the magazine, while Tony wished he was at home, gutting the tiny kitten he had stowed away in his desk drawer. Now, *that* had caused his juvenile penis to twitch in anticipation.

Tony snapped out of his mental trip down memory lane and shot Meadow's pussy a loathsome glare. Without another thought, as she writhed and gagged and made hideous noises, he blasted her box with the bear mace. He even spread the lips of her snatch as far as he could manage and sprayed the remaining contents deep into her vaginal canal. The effects were immediate, and clearly painful. Her twat went crimson as the chemical concoction burnt her tender lady parts like she had douched with battery acid.

"Oh my God, Oh my God, Oh my God, OOOHHH MMMYYY FFFUUUCCCKKKIIINNNGGG GGGOOODDDD!!!!!!!!" Meadow screeched.

Her face bulged like she had been stung by countless wasps. Her eyes continuously wept fluid even though they were swollen shut. Her face looked like it had been dragged across asphalt, raw with road rash.

He sat back and watched in sublime pleasure, Meadow's agonized convulsions a source of pure bliss. Meadow continued to retch and drool and cough and wheeze.

Now that she was fully incapacitated, Tony set about enacting part two of her painful punishment. He stretched her arms out, placing her pretty hands palms up on stout boards, and proceeded to randomly nailgun her fingertips to the wood.

Meadow yowled anew from the fresh hell being bestowed upon her, a wholly bothersome sound that grated on Tony's nerves. He threw a moth-eaten, stained blanket over her head, which muffled her mewling, sort of.

Just as he was about to search for something else to shut her up, all suddenly went silent under the blanket.

"Aww, did you pass out, princess?" Tony teased.

He drove some more nails into Meadow's hands, the metal heads bunched together, bent over one another, causing her digits to look like gnarled branches on a dying tree.

But it wasn't as much fun without her awake to experience it. Tony glared at her blanket-covered head. "Party-pooping bitch…"

Removing the blanket, he went the smelling salts route again, causing Meadow to snap back to consciousness, adrenaline somehow surpassing the pain and allowing her cognitive faculties to take over.

"Please mister… oh god…please stop it…please fucking stop hurting meeeeeeeeeee!"

"That's more like it," he said, commencing to stud her wrists with nail-heads.

But it didn't last long; the pain returned, too

overpowering, and she passed out again, vomiting and nearly choking on it, about to drown in chunks of barf before Tony relented and propped her face, tilting it away from the putrid upchuck.

He maced her again just for the hell of it, her boiled-looking face wet and gleaming from the destructive power of the bear mace, like she had bathed in it.

One of her pinkie fingers had been spared, unnailed to the board, and Tony on impulse seized it in his teeth. He commenced to gnaw it from her distorted hand, incisors chewing through skin and gristle, meeting her proximal phalange and crunching through the slender bone. Wrenching the digit loose, he deposited it in his front pocket to save for later.

Tony then grabbed the nail gun again and opened fire at Meadow's bounteous breasts. The sharp steel penetrated her nipples easily, splitting it like a hotdog in the microwave. The large soft mounds of her mammary glands, studded with nail-heads, seeped blood over her chest and stomach. Always battling with his OCD, he did his best to deliver an even number of nails to each breast.

Seeing her right nipple was still unscathed, he bit it off too. A soft tearing sound reached his ears as he tore at the taut and stretched breast tissue with his teeth. Shreds of gristle and areola remnants were embedded between his incisors by the time the nipple ripped free.

Chewing thoughtfully, he observed the incoherent, babbling ruin that had once been a lively teenage girl. Almost as an afterthought, he fired a quick succession of nails into her sphincter, and crisscrossed some through her ass meat,

Chapter 11

Sanded Faceless

Hardware Tony was unsurprised to see everyone fully awake and agitated in the next room.

The Ricci family, according to Paulie, consisted of Brandon Ricci himself, his archaic father, his wife Charmaine, and his hellion son AJ. Being chained and in an obviously dire situation didn't stop them from bickering amongst themselves, until they noticed him watching them from the entryway.

Furio, the elderly patriarch, craned his head in Tony's direction. "Hey you! Big man! Yeah, you! Come untie me from this chair. Respect your goddamned elders!"

"Dad, shut the fuck up!" Brandon said. "Don't berate the guy who's here to kill us!"

"He will not," said AJ. "Cause you're gonna bust loose and kick his ass, right, Daddy?"

"AJ, baby, stop ... Your worthless, no-good father got us *into* this mess," Charmaine spat.

"Jesus Christ, maybe death *is* better ..." Brandon moaned.

Tony took in the fractured family dynamics and smiled in good-natured mirth. It would be fun killing such hateful people. They were like weeds to be plucked from a well-maintained garden.

"Everyone just needs to relax," he told them. "I will get to each of you in due time. I am a professional in the art of gore, and I take that job extremely seriously."

"You're fucking insane!" Charmaine screeched.

"No, ma'am, I'm totally lucid ... for the most part. Now, when it comes to my work and the pride I take in it, I can fully admit that my mind goes to another plane of existence. One where demons reside, demons who tell me what to do to the sheep that I slaughter. I get my orders straight from Hell itself."

They stared at him in absolute shock, and he supposed the sight of him didn't help. He was covered in blood and other bodily fluids, talking demonic entities. No wonder they thought he was insane.

Maybe so, maybe no. But what he *was*, was a professional. The forged steel restraints shackling them should have told them that.

Maybe they were thinking they could try and escape his nefarious grasp, but how? Maybe they imagined somebody from the outside would come to rescue them.

Both scenarios, Tony knew, were hopelessly futile, but one of the biggest flaws in the human psyche is the notion of clinging to hope even when there isn't any. Every one of the Ricci's chose to ignore logic and clung to that hope like a drowning person desperately holding onto a buoy in a churning, violent sea.

"Now," he said, "I've already decided the roster, and victim number one will be ..." He mimed a drum roll. "Furio! Congrats, Pops, you're up first!"

"What the hell are your plans with me, sonny? You gonna shoot a helpless old man? A sick old man who's got emphysema?" Furio demanded.

The prissy look of distaste that etched itself onto Tony's broad face might have been almost comical under other circumstances.

"Please," he scoffed, affronted. "Guns are for heathens, stickup men, and lowlife hoodlums. Like your son! I create *art*! Art through blood, gore, and tools. Demean me like that again, and you'll get a hammer to the face!"

All of them, convinced, quickly shut their traps. Seeing someone like him become enraged, Tony knew, was a truly scary spectacle. They had to be thinking it was best to keep this ticking time bomb at bay–try not to rile him up any more than necessary.

After Tony composed himself, he went to his workstation, grabbed an item, and returned to Furio.

"Since you asked about my plan," he said, "this is a BAXTER6 Professional Orbital Composite Air Sander. One of the best models on the market right now."

"And what are you going to do with it?" Furio croaked.

"Isn't it obvious, old timer? I'm going to sand you faceless!"

The response was immediate, screams and outcries filling the room, as might be expected. Tony took in their cacophony of despair like a priest in confessional, before looking Furio dead in his cataract-covered orbs.

To his credit, the geriatric geezer did not look away, attempting to stare Tony down. He must have been one tough S.O.B. in his prime, but now he was just a bag of loose skin and bones. Killing him was, really, the ultimate favor. Giving him the respect, he deserved.

He whirred the machine to life and, like a switch was thrown, all resolve left Furio. He flinched away, whining, "Hey, wait a minute, sonny … aren't you going to give me any last words?"

"I just did, old man."

With that, Tony brought the sander to Furio's cheek. His paper-thin, liver-spotted skin gave way instantly, peeling off like the rind of an orange. Blood ran freely as his cheek was shredded and abraded down to gleaming bone.

The others went nuts again, but he tuned them out, moving on to the old man's chin. The strength of the sander could not be contested; it ate through the old man's flesh like butter, shredding his face into bloody ribbons. Tendrils of smoke plumed from the friction of sandpaper against bone.

***

Brandon yelled in horror at his father's fractured features, but, in all honesty, he didn't care if the old bastard died.

Furio had been a real piece of work, nearly all of Brandon's life, priding himself on severe discipline, seeming to take great delight in bare bottom spankings with his weathered, leather belt, sometimes gouging tender ass-cheeks with the tarnished metal buckle.

So, if this big fat Guido wanted to remove his pop's face, then, as far as Brandon was concerned, he could have at it.

He didn't much care about his wife either. She had bloated into a fat bitch after they married, and guarded her pussy like it was Fort Knox.

AJ, though … Brandon looked at his son, seeing the tears

73

dribbling from his eyes, and his heart went out to the boy. AJ was the only family member -- hell, the only *person* -- he cared for.

Maybe, just maybe, he could somehow get out of his shackles and rescue his son before it was too late.

Furio's screams of torment tore Brandon from his feverish thoughts and brought him back to the here and now. The belt sander chewed away the old man's lips, ejecting them to the side in gory chunks of misshapen flesh, leaving a ghoulish permanent grin of exposed teeth ... what few of them remained. A gurgled mesh of words drowning in a sea of clotted blood vomited from Furio's mouth. Applying force at an awkward but effective angle, Hardware Tony ground his tongue into a paste of flesh, leaving only an undulating nub.

Furio's head fell back, as if it suddenly felt too heavy to hold upright. His glassy eyes stared up at the fluorescent lights in the ceiling. Tony, leering jackal-like, pressed the unforgiving sander into his face full force, spraying gore every which way possible. The sander mulched up Furio's eyes and regurgitated them into the air in a gluey mush, intermixed with a fine mist of ruby red. Furio's sightless face began to shake violently, the ropy stalks of springy optic nerves waggling from their sockets like nightmare cuckoo clocks from Hell.

***

Engrossed in his work, Tony barely noticed Furio's passing. He was too intent on waging war on the old man's face. He sanded off an ear, first tearing it in half before adding even more torque and shredding it into a goopy glob of unrecognizable clumps, then reciprocated on the other ear with the same cruel treatment. The sander carried on belching out a torrent of gruel as it reduced the flesh into pulpy soup. Furio's visage had taken on the characteristics of a grilled cheese on a piping hot griddle.

He didn't stop making mincemeat out of the cadaverous old fuck until the professional grade sandpaper tore away from the sander due to overuse. By then, Furio's face was nonexistent. It looked like an IED had detonated, leaving a tunneled crater in place of facial features. His body dangled limply from the examination chair; blood puddled pleasantly on the gore strewn concrete below.

The remaining Ricci's collectively lost their shit again. They had been dumped into a living nightmare with no means to wake up. The contrast between them and Hardware Tony was the difference between night and day; he was living his best life; a brilliant smile beaming from his blood-smeared face. He eagerly clapped his gory hands in anticipation of the next kill.

Observing Charmaine's nude body with a clinical eye, he noted her arms had collected some extra fat, as had her thighs and belly. Stretch marks adorned nearly every area of her body. A large thatch of curly, black pubic hair obscured most of her crotch. Her ass was rotund, with a slight cottage cheese look to it, but nothing too revolting.

A shame she had let her body go. He wasn't into the female form in that way, but her face was still beautiful, and she had amazing DD breasts. He pondered what she had looked like in her twenties. Probably a knockout.

"I could lie and say I hate to be the bearer of bad news," he said, "but this is a place of honesty. And, while it may be bad news for you, for me it's the best news possible. I have yet another toy to put to use in a gloriously spectacular fashion! And I get to share it with your family!"

"You're sick!" Charmaine screamed. "You're a demented piece of shit!"

"Maybe you're right." He shrugged. "But, for me, it's the only way I know how to be. This is all very normal in my book."

"Mommy … I want to go home! He killed Grampa! I'm scared!" sniffled AJ.

"I know baby … I want to go home too!"

"Money," Brandon said, desperately. "I have money. How does ten-thousand dollars sound?"

Tony felt rage rapidly building in his brain.

These pathetic wretches always thought they could compromise his integrity with *money*. How? He had all the money he needed. He was paid handsomely, and spent very little on things that didn't have a purpose for his art. A decent TV, an array of books and DVDs, but otherwise that was about it for possessions.

Brandon looked imploringly at Tony, waiting for his rebuttal. "So … Uh … how does that sound?" he reiterated.

"It sounds … like a bribe," Tony said. "And I don't take bribes! You're going to pay for insulting me!"

"I'm sorry! Just forget I mentioned it!"

"Fuck you! You think, because you have money, you're above the law? Well guess what? I'm the law here. I'm the judge, jury, and executioner. You have ensured your place in

Hell, and I'm going to send you there!"

He stepped back and took a breath.

"But first," he went on, "I'm going to make you all suffer to the fullest. And your pig wife is next!"

Chapter 12

Chainsaw Cunt-Fuck

Anger was a detriment. It could cause him to kill his victims too fast, and that would be a highly regrettable mistake.

No, he needed a level head now, because he was about to have some real fun. He had picked some truly gnarly ways to die for the remaining members of the Ricci clan. The warehouse was going to need a deep cleaning when he was done, there was no doubt about it!

The Husqvarna 3120 XP was truly the Cadillac of chainsaws. a professional 119CC, built for felling the largest of trees in the world, it was the most powerful one on the planet. It could pull the chain on even the longest bar, which was six feet!

Charmaine had been clamped into an Avante Milano OB50 OB/GYN Procedure Table. The top-of-the-line gynecological examination chair had cost Tony over seven thousand dollars, but was worth every penny. He quickly and efficiently placed Charmaine's feet into the stirrups, spreading her legs and allowing for easy access to her middle-aged vagina.

Once again, he had the arduous task of looking into the yawning cavern of another worthless cunt. It was alright though; this one was only moments away from being eviscerated by the gleaming teeth of the chainsaw's unforgiving blade.

Tony took another long, hard look at Charmaine, before turning his gaze to the others. AJ was crying and trying his best not to look at his mother's nude form. His face was crimson in embarrassment and fear. Brandon had that thousand-yard stare Tony had seen countless times before, like he was on another plane of existence.

It was kind of a mind trick a person plays on themselves when their brain can't handle the pickle, they have found themselves in. But pain would eradicate the false sense of security Brandon's brain had temporarily created soon enough. If seeing what happened to Charmaine didn't affect him strongly enough, the plan Tony had for little AJ would surely do the job.

Tony chuckled to himself as he pictured the bloodbath playing out in his diseased mind. He returned his searing gaze to Charmaine, who shrank back into the chair in terror, begging and whimpering piteously.

Without activating the saw, Tony hefted it and guided the chain of teeth along Charmaine's inner thighs, then lightly brushed her clitoris, nicking it in the process and creating a bloom of blood on its ultra-sensitive tip. Charmaine shrieked and struggled in her seat, like she would be able to escape her bonds, but there was no escaping this.

He guided the chainsaw to within inches of the precipice of her pussy before engaging the pull start and gripping the throttle. The engine chugged to life and evened out into a steady roar. Charmaine's eyes bulged as the spinning blade of the chain edged closer to her delicate lady parts.

"PLEASE GOD NO! OH MY GOD, OH MY GOD,

SOMEBODY HELP MEEEEEEE!"

Unfortunately for Charmaine, her pleas for amnesty fell upon deaf ears. Pain was the master here, not clemency.

"Prepare for insertion in ... 3-2-1-go!"

"NNNOOO!!!!"

That was what she got out before he shoved the chainsaw blade into her vaginal entrance. The meat of her cunt instantly sliced into ribbons, hurling liquid chunks violently into Tony's chest with a wet *smacking* sound as he cranked the throttle to the max speed. Blood gushed out at an astounding rate while portions of ground up, minced entrails expelled out of the flared orifice. More blood, blacker than freshly laid tar, spouted from Charmaine's twisted jaws as she shrieked in torment.

"YYYAAARRRGGGHHH!!!!"

The bisecting blade continued its upward ascent, carving deeply into her shredded guts like a tunneling mole, plowing through her malleable, avulsed flesh. The commanding steel chopped up the large and small intestine and demolished her ruptured stomach, ravenously gnawing away at the sturdy organ, splitting it in half and spewing out the partially digested remnants of her last meal.

The next casualty for the relentless saw was the gallbladder. A violent stream of greenish-yellow bile coated the inside of Charmaine's partially hollowed out body cavity. She was tattooed in her own digestive fluids.

By now, she was clearly dead, but that didn't deter Tony from his Missouri chainsaw massacre on her remains. The blade sheared up out of her torso between her hanging, heavy, pale breasts, slinging out bits of mangled spleen and liver.

Having basically sawed her in half lengthwise, from crotch to collarbones, Tony killed the engine and set the smoking, bloody weapon on the table next to the murdered matriarch.

Brandon must have been hollering the whole time, but Tony had hardly noticed over the chainsaw's buzzing roar and the sounds of its blades grinding through flesh and bone. Now, in the relative quiet, he caught some of the man's frantic raving.

"You fucking piece of dogshit! Killing my boy's mother right in front of him!?! I'm gonna rip your head off with my bare hands!"

AJ, meanwhile, only stared at the floor as if desperately attempting to ignore the eviscerated carcass next to him that used to be his doting, loving mom. Now her insides hung outside her emptied cadaver in a gushy pile of innards and gore.

Brandon continued boiling belligerently in his chair, ranting and raving, trapped in his restraints as his fury-fueled mind vowing to slaughter Hardware Tony. Tony magnanimously let him go on until he lost steam, but then, AJ went off.

"You killed my momma! She never hurt nobody! You're a bad, bad, man!"

"Well, kiddo, your daddy needed to be taught a lesson about forcing his loved ones into aiding and abetting his nefarious life choices," Tony said.

"He didn't force me! I wanted to help!"

"You actually *wanted* to help your dad rob and kill

somebody?" Tony asked.

"It was *me* that got the driver to stop!" AJ boasted. "I want to be just like my dad when I grow up!" He threw an adoring hero-worship look at Brandon, who returned a tentative smile.

That smile quickly faded as Brandon looked at Tony, the cogs of whose mind were working over what AJ, in his pride and naïveté, had just said. The boy might have gotten a quick, painless death, till he opened his mouth, and Brandon surely knew little AJ had just sealed his own gruesome fate.

"Well shit, AJ," Tony said. "This changes everything! I was just going to kill you and get it over with, since I assumed you were innocent of this whole sordid business. I must be getting tenderhearted or foolish in my old age!" He laughed. "But no one is ever truly innocent, are they? You sure proved that!"

***

Brandon saw it dawn on his son, the mistake he had made, and the levels of deep shit they were wading through. Whining like a wounded puppy, AJ uselessly yanked at his shackles, fear's cold, bony hand no doubt grasping his tiny, racing heart and beginning to squeeze. He cast a plaintive glance at his father, searching for some kind of solace, but Brandon could only muster a grim, determined, grimace.

The situation was akin to the ISIS videos he had watched on Rotten.com a few weeks back. Just a bunch of doomed men, waiting to be murdered on camera to enrage all the other nations when they viewed the extreme propaganda videos.

He watched Hardware Tony, deep in contemplation, pacing the floor while muttering to himself, like the lunatic he truly was. After he finished his one-sided argument, he snapped his head up and turned to the remaining Ricci's with an officious smirk.

"Since you truly seem determined to follow in your father's footsteps even at this alarmingly young age," Tony said to AJ, "I think it proves the tried-and-true adage of *the apple doesn't fall far from the tree*."

"Leave him alone," Brandon pleaded. "Come on, he's just a kid; he doesn't know any better!"

Tony ignored him, still focused on AJ. "There's clearly no point in showing you leniency. As a matter of fact, I think I ought to teach you a lesson."

AJ quivered. "What are you going to do?"

"Good question." He paced some more, hemming and hawing thoughtfully. "Now, a child your age, who has no remorse for helping his father rob and kill an innocent man ... that may make you a loyal son, but it also makes you a real piece of shit. A thoroughly shitty human being in general. And, for that, I have a most fitting, and truly special, penance in mind for you."

Chapter 13

Diarrhea Waterboarding

"Let me ask you a question, AJ. Are you familiar with waterboarding?"

AJ, feeling like a deer caught in the headlights of an oncoming car, slowly shook his head.

"Well then, allow me to explain!" Tony said, as cheerfully as if on a television show. "Waterboarding is a form of torture in which a person is tied to a board, tilted backward at an incline of about 0 to 20 degrees." He angled his hand to demonstrate. "The person's face is covered with a cloth, which means they can't see, so they don't know when it's going to happen. Then, water is poured over the cloth, flooding the person's breathing passages, causing them to experience the sensation of drowning."

At first, it didn't sound so bad. Just someone having water poured over their face, big deal. But, as the appalling man elaborated, the reality of what he was describing started to sink in.

"Normally, the water is poured intermittently, giving the person a chance to gasp for breath, prolonging the torture. Other times, it's poured uninterruptedly, not letting them breathe at all. Waterboarding causes extreme pain, damage to the lungs and brain from oxygen deprivation, the possibility of other physical injuries including broken bones due to struggling against restraints, and lasting psychological damage to those who survive it."

AJ began to cry in earnest. Waterboarding sounded *terrifying*. That someone could be drowned like that, even in the dry relative "safety" of this hellacious warehouse, as easily as they could be drowned in a lake or the ocean? He hated swimming anyway, was deathly afraid of the water, and had been since his dad let him watch *Jaws*. The water was not only dangerous in terms of drowning, but it also housed a vast menagerie of deadly creatures in its murky depths, especially sharks!

"Please, mister, don't!" AJ cried. "I'm scared of the water!"

"Oh, don't fret, my boy," Tony said. "I'm not going to use water on you."

AJ relaxed a little; maybe the man was just messing with him. Maybe, despite what had happened to his mom, it was going to be okay.

"Since you're nothing but a little shit," he went on, with a cruel grin, "I have something special I've been saving up for just such an occasion! Be right back!"

He ran off, leaving AJ to wonder what was going to happen. He glanced at his dad for reassurance, but his dad slumped in the chair, not even trying to pull at the handcuffs, like he was bracing himself for something even more horrible that what they'd already seen.

Hardware Tony waltzed back in with a sealed five-gallon bucket that sloshed loudly as it swayed back and forth in his grip. He placed the bucket on the floor next to AJ.

"See, I wanted to use something that mimicked exactly how you are as an individual," he said. "And I thought to myself, well, there's the saying 'sweets for the sweet' ... so, why not 'shits for the shit'?"

He popped the lid on the bucket. The stench was so bad, AJ's eyes watered, and he horked like he was about to throw up. It was poop, but it was a thousand times worse than just regular poop. It was the worst poop in the world, a hot and festering reek like nothing he could ever have imagined.

It even brought his dad around with a revolted cry. "Jesus fucking *Christ*!"

Tony didn't seem bothered by it at all. He rocked the bucket some more, sloshing the semi-liquified, nasty stew. "And," he said, "just in case waterboarding with diarrhea wasn't bad enough, how about diarrhea allowed to ferment a good long time in the summer heat? You know how bad the humidity gets around here!"

"What kind of nutjob keeps a bucket of rancid *shit* sitting around?" choked his dad, dry-heaving.

The fiend didn't answer him, his evil grin fixed on AJ. "But even that wasn't enough for *me*, my little buckaroo! No siree! I added a nice little surprise before I sealed it up, to make it extra special!"

He stirred the bucket's contents with a yardstick, a poisonous fog of putrescence rising from the malodorous pail. AJ did throw up then, all down his front, and his eyes were watering so badly he could hardly see.

"Daddy, help meeeee!" he wailed.

But his dad was too busy also throwing up to reply.

Tony tipped AJ's chair backward, so the child's feet were higher than his head A few seconds later, the horrible man's cheerful face hovered above him. "Would you like to know what the secret ingredient is?"

"No! I want to go home!"

"Now, don't be like that. Of course, you want to know!" The dreadful man dunked his hand to the elbow, making gross squelching noises as he fished around. "Aha!" he cried triumphantly, lifting something out.

Something rotten and slimy that, to AJ, looked a whole lot like a dead baby.

***

The putrid infant corpse, raised from the vile vessel of its resting place, was indeed quite a sight. Black and green blotches covered its bloated, shiny skin. Its deteriorating flesh seethed with maggots. Some fell from it, raining back into the bucket with a host of tiny splashes.

It felt, in Tony's hand, as sloppy and disgusting as it looked, with a loose and squishy slippery texture. Bacteria had obviously grown and flourished. The softened, decaying meat seemed about to slough right off the small, fragile bones.

One tiny baby eyeball hung low out of a gooey socket, glistening, reminiscent of an overripe cherry oozing juices. Chunks had been gnawed from its rump and thighs, leaving grisly craters. Various cuts and scrapes oozed brownish fluids. Its slack, toothless mouth drooled rivulets of liquified shit.

The stub of a yellow #2 pencil jutted from the newborn's diminutive sphincter. The casual onlooker might not be able to tell if the infant had been sodomized by the writing instrument before, or after, its pitiful death ... only Hardware

Tony knew, and he wasn't telling.

Smiling wickedly to his captive audience, Tony dropped the corpse back into its marinade of shit stew. He hefted the bucket onto the table beside AJ and picked up a towel that looked like it had been moonlighting as a re-used maxi pad for a week straight.

"I'm going to get you for this, you callous son-of-a-bitch!" Brandon said, his voice clogged with puke. "When I do, I'll be the one torturing *your* ass!"

"I'm shaking in my boots," Tony told him. "My track record for escapees is flawless … not lost one yet! If you want to be the first, please, feel free to try! Now, if you'll excuse me, I really need to begin this procedure. *Tempus fugit*, and all that."

He moved toward AJ, shaking out the dried, crusty towel. The boy immediately began squirming and sniveling.

"No no no, don't put that on me, no!"

After verifying that the boy was still securely bound and in position, Tony draped his head with the revolting rag, despite his pleas.

Then, he dipped a metal canteen cup into the mire of muck and poured it slowly onto the towel. It spread and soaked in, gradually saturating the cloth, as AJ uttered muffled gags and sobs.

Tony went on applying the tepid room-temperature shit-stew in a steady, controlled manner. He was glad he'd had the foresight to save it up; one never knew what might come in handy in his line of work. The diarrhea mélange had been collected from various victims during their visits to his warehouse and ranged from the watery and acidic kind to the thick and gooey kind. Some had the consistency of peanut butter, some included partial soft turds that began to dissolve once they were ejected from a gaping, reddened, shit speckled asshole. Even a few more solid corn-cakers had made the mix, adding a particular lumpiness.

With the towel soaked in moldering mess, and completely covering both AJ's mouth and nose, his air flow was greatly restricted. And what air he could get was permeated with feculent fecal matter, giving him no choice but to breathe it in. He paused a few times to move the towel away from the kid's beet-colored, brown-smeared face, giving him a chance to catch an unimpeded inhalation, before resuming the procedure.

All the while, Brandon kept up his litany of futile threats, but it was only background music to Tony's ears. He ladled on the loathsome liquid like pancake batter, until a sick and delightful idea struck with brusque force.

AJ got a somewhat longer reprieve from the deluge, though the towel was left draped soddenly over his head as Tony dug around in the bucket's gory gunk. Again, pulling out the maggoty infant monstrosity, he plopped it onto his worktable, found an old well-used rolling pin, and set to flattening the gooshy corpse as best as he could.

The sound of small breaking bones bore a striking resemblance to popping bacon grease in a skillet. Biological gruel squeezed out of the cadaver's orifices like a perforated toothpaste tube being squeezed. When it resembled a rubbery, misshapen bath mat, Tony laid it across and atop the towel covering little AJ's face.

"Alright, kiddo," he announced cheerily, "Here comes

round two!"

He recommenced dipping the shit-encrusted canteen cup back into the bucket's squalid contents and pouring it liberally onto the boy's diarrhea-drenched face. A veritable shit tsunami of countless consistencies coursed down the sides of his head.

AJ's lower body twitched from the lack of oxygen, as well as abhorrent disgust. As if in an act of defiance, he pissed his pants, the hot buttery-tinted fluid creating an ever-widening puddle of piss, trickling up his inverted body, funneling onto the chair, and sprinkling the floor below him.

The stench under the rag had to be unbearable, yes, but the fact that the dank slop was also able to inundate and soak through the fabric was the real game changer. Not only was the smell having its effect and the waterboarding process itself impeding his air intake... the deluge of corrupted crap seeped into his mouth. This, clearly, proved to be truly too much to take. AJ began violently vomiting, but with his head covered by the limp weight of the towel and a flattened, baby corpse, his regurgitated chunks had nowhere to go.

The kid was convulsing, drowning in excrement and choking on puke, mere seconds from blacking out, when Tony abruptly yanked the suffocating layers away.

AJ turned his filthy, plum-colored face to the side and expelled an audacious amount of moldering manure that had been clogging his inflamed throat. A downpour of shit pushed from his lips like a malfunctioning soft serve ice cream machine, while more snorted from his clogged nostrils. Finally clearing his mouth, AJ gasped gusts of air into his fiery, depleted lungs.

***

Brandon stared in anguish at his writhing child. He wished he could go to AJ and give him the comfort he so desperately needed.

He then cast his caustic gaze at Hardware Tony, and wished upon everything holy he could somehow get his hooks into that cold-hearted bastard. He would annihilate Tony in a heartbeat.

You could never discount a person with absolutely zero to lose; it made them unpredictable and dangerous, and that's how Brandon perceived himself. He felt lethal and on the verge of a murderous frenzy.

His bravado quickly waned as reality harshly lashed out and reminded him of the winless situation he had been cast into. Unless a *deus ex machina* was heading Brandon's way, life was essentially over for him and his son.

With an almost indiscernible quickness, Hardware Tony had AJ unshackled and dragged the sputtering boy to the floor, securing him cruciform-style to ring-bolt restraints embedded in the concrete.

Brandon could only launch another tirade of verbal abuse, pelting words at Hardware Tony like fists from a powerful pugilist.

"You're lucky you have me locked up, you fucking coward cocksucker, otherwise I would tear you limb from fucking limb! The first chance I get; I am going to stomp a mudhole in your fat ass!"

Tony only laughed.

"Oh, settle down," he chided. "Don't make me remove both of your eyes with an ice cream scooper! If I do that, how will you be able to see me finish the job on your bratty kid?"

"W-W-What?" Brandon asked.

"I'm sorry, did you assume *that* was his maximum punishment? A token shit-shower, and then all done, away he goes, safe and sound? Please! Give me *some* credit, here!"

He trotted off to some other corner of the ungodly warehouse, leaving Brandon trapped in his chair and AJ having exhausted hysterics chained to the floor.

When he returned moments later, he was pushing a Honda HRX 217VKA, one of the most expensive and powerful self-propelled gas mowers on the market.

Chapter 14

Mulched By the Mower

"Are you fucking kidding me?" Brandon yelled, as his stunned, horrified brain finally caught up with his tongue.

Hardware Tony tutted. "I think by now you know the answer to that." He started the mower. Its snarling bellow was deafening in the enclosed space.

AJ's bloodshot eyes bulged in bewilderment from his shit- and puke-caked little face. He could only watch with the helplessness of someone caught in a reoccurring nightmare as Tony menacingly pushed the mower closer and closer. There was no more fight left within the cringing child; it had been effectively wrenched from him over the course of the evening.

His father, though, still had vitriol profusely pumping in his system. He furiously pulled at his restraints, the attempt only causing the flesh at his wrists to tear and weep blood. Nonetheless, Hardware Tony had to hand it to the doomed man; such anger was truly a gift, and it fueled him longer than anyone else who had sat in one of these chairs, waiting their turn. In that aspect, Brandon was a rarity, like an unexpected archaeological find.

Tony was excited to see how Brandon would react to the torture method in store for him. One thing was certain: at least he wouldn't just roll over like a defeated opponent and take his punishment, like all the others Tony had sent to their doom.

He was getting ahead of himself, though! First up was this malcontented child, already well on his way to hooliganism.

AJ lay pinned to the ground by his restraints, as he writhed and wiggled in a desperate attempt at trying to escape his fate. It was the truest form of desperation, its very definition. There was no escaping this. Even if AJ hadn't been part of his father's transgressions, Tony would have eventually found him regardless and extinguished the light in the boy's fearful eyes. Some things were all inevitable in the end.

"I'm going to start at your feet, kiddo," he told him, speaking almost kindly. "Can't make it too quick, now, can we? I want your agony to last for as long as humanly possible."

AJ didn't answer, eyes scrunched shut in absolute terror like an unending, living nightmare he was enduring.

"I feel sorry for your mother," Brandon muttered, "for raising a fucking monster like you."

This bit of rancor surprisingly struck a nerve with Tony. Usually, his potential victims' taunts left him unfazed, but his mother was a very sore subject.

"You feel sorry for *my* mother, huh?" He turned off the lawnmower and stalked toward Brandon "Well, allow me to explain why you shouldn't waste one iota of brain strength on *that* worthless, droning insect."

Brandon held his gaze with a malignant glare. Now that one of his barbs had gotten through, he would have to see what kind of fruit this strange tree would bear. Maybe anger might cloud Tony's judgment, making him slip up, and allowing Brandon to somehow get the upper hand.

The slick consistency of the blood dribbling from his ruined wrists was reminiscent of motor oil. Brandon thought that, if he had to, he could maybe deglove himself. It would hurt like a bitch but would be worth it if he could get out of this jam. Although his wrists were already killing him, he kept working them, twisting them back and forth, feeling the skin part and give way.

"My mother was a … complicated woman," Tony said.

So far, he appeared oblivious to Brandon's efforts at escaping his shackles. The key was to keep him talking, and if his mother was a sore spot, then so be it.

"Oh, yeah, I bet," he said, sneering. "Boo Hoo, mommy issues."

Tony glared at Brandon with contempt. "She was! She loved drugs, alcohol, and sex, not always in that order. I was just the vestige of an unhappy relationship, the unwanted gift of a sperm donor. I tried my best to avoid her ire, because it always brought punishment. She would pinch my genitals and put out lit cigarettes on the tip of my penis. She always said that a man's cock was the root of all evil, and that every male should have his dick and balls removed so he could be a eunuch."

Seeing his face flush and his fists clench, Brandon dared to hope the big butcher would goad himself into a heart attack or a stroke. If him dropping dead meant having to forego exacting a slow and torturous revenge, well, Brandon decided he would be okay with that.

"She used to threaten me with that fate when I was younger," Tony said, eyes dark with bad memories. "When she was on a bender, she would chase me throughout the house with a pair of gardening shears! Is it any wonder I started hating women? They were all like her, even the little girls. I started to take out my aggressions on them whenever I could. Each one of my victims would morph into my mother as I killed them."

"Yeah, some tough guy, going after little girls." He tugged surreptitiously at the manacles, trying not to wince from the pain as the skin of his wrists began to bunch and slide. the raw, red flesh beneath wept tears of blood.

"Then she caught me." Tony spoke as if from far away. "Grace Budd, the girl's name was. Fourteen years old. I was making her ejaculate blood and cutting pieces out of her body. I didn't even know anyone else was in the room until I heard a husky sigh and turned around to see my mother."

He shuddered from head to toe, and something in his expression made Brandon bite back another round of snide remarks.

"Naked," he said, making a sick sound. "Naked and pleasuring herself while she watched, her vein-laden, liver spotted hand pawing at her cunt, her pubic hair matted with vaginal fluid."

"Shit," murmured Brandon, taken aback.

Tony began to march around the room, waving his arms and fighting for composure. This was clearly a difficult subject for him, and Brandon was glad. Not only did it give him more time to strain at the manacles, it obviously caused Tony a great deal of distress and pain. Which, in Brandon's humble opinion, the murderous cocksucker most definitely deserved.

"She didn't say a word. Neither did I. We never talked about it. Later that night, when she was asleep, I went into her room with a claw hammer and my trusty penknife."

His faraway gaze mellowed to an almost nostalgic quality.

"The sound the hammer made as it cracked her skull ... the way bits of her diseased brain bulged out ..." He sighed, somewhat wistfully. "I cut off her head with the penknife. It took forever, hacking and sawing, but I did it. Then I placed it on a shelf, where I screamed and swore at and taunted it. I threw darts at it, paying particular attention to the eyeballs, since the eyes are windows into the soul, or so they say. I guess I was trying to destroy her spirit with those pointy projectiles."

On the floor, AJ listened, rapt and aghast. Brandon felt much the same. Matricide had to be one of the worst kinds of crimes. How could someone kill the very person who had granted your life? A mother was a boy's best friend. AJ knew that; everyone knew that.

Brandon couldn't think of a lower piece of shit than a mother killer. They were worse than pedophiles, in his mind.

Tony chuckled, a little ruefully. "When the dart game became boring, I cut out her tongue and larynx and shoved them down the garbage disposal. The disposal was supposed to be rated for chicken bones, but, for whatever reason, it couldn't handle her vocal cords. Too tough and stringy, maybe? I don't know. I hammered the rest of her head to a pulp, walked out the door, and never looked back."

Brandon's mouth had gone dry; Hardware Tony was even more of a psycho than the rumors would have it, more of a psycho than he'd already demonstrated right here in this warehouse tonight.

"So," Tony said, exhaling gustily. He turned a wry grin on Brandon. "You want to try and psychoanalyze me? You think I've got mommy issues? Fine. Whatever. I also have kid-killing issues, as you are about to witness."

The lawnmower's engine roared back to life. Brandon and AJ screamed and pleaded in unison as Tony steered it towards AJ's feet. He hefted on the handle, raising the mower's back wheels into the air. The spinning, sharpened blades twirled frenetically above his quivering toes.

"PLEASE! MISTER! NO! NO! NO! NO! NO! DADDY, PLEASE HELP MEEEEE!!!!" AJ gibbered.

Brandon howled in a combination of rage intermingled with earth-shattering sorrow. Despite his best efforts, his bloodied wrists and half-skinned hands were still lodged in the shackles. He could only helplessly watch the terrible events unfold in front of his unbelieving eyes.

The whirling steel blades sent severed toes skittering in ten different directions. AJ's cries hit a note that should have shattered glass. Tony allowed the mower to drop onto the rest of his feet. The damage was instant and severe. Blood, flesh, and shards of bone flew everywhere.

The sound of metal versus meat was explicit. to be sure, but the noises AJ made took the cake. Brandon's own screams were not far behind.

Tony, jaw set like a landscaper taking on a challenging thicket of brambles, forced the mower onward and upward. The machine struggled a little, balking and chugging, as its blades met the stouter shinbones, but gamely continued, even when the spinning steel struck loud clangs and bright sparks from the chains at AJ's ankles.

"Dadd-eeeeeee!" he keened, his legs a mulched mess from the knees down.

It seemed like some form of sorcery to Brandon's reeling mind. His son, being erased from existence before his very eyes. He wept, as impotent to save his son as he had been Charmaine, and his own father. Impotent, even, to save his own miserable life.

"Pleeeeeease, God!" screeched AJ, evidently giving up on Daddy with a resignation that sent daggers of shame stabbing into Brandon's heart. "Please God kill the bad man, make him die, make him go away!"

Nothing happened to Tony.

God.

Did.

Nothing.

At.

All.

No miracles. No divine intervention. No sudden walloping massive heart attack or stroke to end Tony's cruelty.

Instead, as AJ's shrieks became incomprehensible gurgles, Tony kept pushing the lawnmower further and further up his feebly-spasming body. The blades sheared away the meat of AJ's thighs, julienning the arteries, grinding away at the thick femurs.

AJ made no more noise and had stopped moving by the time the mower chewed its way over his pre-adolescent groin, but Tony was nowhere near finished, AJ's midsection was next, guts laid open, chopped intestines messily flung about.

Then his chest, the skin flayed apart to expose ribs. A haze of blood splatter hung in the air.

Last but not least, Tony brought the gore-encased mower to AJ's head. With a triumphant sneer at Brandon, he lowered the spinning, chopping blades onto AJ's face, pulpifying it on contact, the edges stripping the meat away in an instant, spitting bloody scraps of AJ's scalp from the side discharge of the mower. Blood decanted from every portion of AJ, pooling widely around him.

Only when Tony raised and dropped the mower again, causing the blade to bite deeply into the skull and lodge there, did the engine blat and sputter out. Swearing, Tony yanked the stalled machine from the boy's body and tugged at the cord, trying to restart it.

"That's enough," sobbed Brandon brokenly. "Jesus, he's dead, okay? Isn't that what you wanted? That's enough!"

Another hard tug brought the mower back to life. Tony's satisfaction was unmistakable as he dropped the whirling blades back onto AJ's head. This time, they easily shattered his compromised skull, leaving a massive, gaping hole that showcased his brain ... before the mower pulverized that, too, shooting red-streaked grayish mush with such great force, some of it hit the far wall with a meaty splat.

Finally satisfied, Tony heaved the mower off AJ's pathetic remains and trundled the crimson-caked death machine toward a far corner of the warehouse. Its tires left an expansive trail of gore in its departing wake.

For Brandon, it was now or never. He had one hand about halfway degloved and was a moment away from freeing his wrist from its restraints when Tony turned, saw him, and broke into a lumbering run.

Despite his size, Tony was fast, reaching Brandon just as that one crumple-skinned, flensed appendage slipped free. His other hand still trapped, Brandon took a wild swing, which ended as Tony caught his blood-slicked forearm in both brutish fists and snapped the bones like a bundle of dry spaghetti noodles.

Brandon howled in white hot agony. He howled three more times, as Tony battered his other wrist and then both his ankles. Even if he could have gotten out of the chair, a crippled-crab scrabble would have been the best he could hope for.

"Did you really think I wouldn't notice what you were up to?" Tony teased.

Brandon only rocked his pain-stricken body in stunned silence; grief and agony had robbed him of his vernacular.

Nor could he find the words to say anything a few minutes later, when Tony, having vanished, returned driving an ATV. The trailer behind it carried a large, bulky tarp-covered object. He parked near Brandon's chair and dismounted.

"Now, then," he said, sounding pleased with himself. "It's finally your turn, Daddy-O! And I saved, if not the *best* for last, at least the one with the most style to it!"

With all the flourish of a discount stage magician, Tony whisked off the tarp, revealing what lay beneath it to

Brandon's dismayed gaze.

A woodchipper.

Of course, it just *had* to be a fucking woodchipper …

Chapter 15

How Much Flesh Would a Woodchipper Chip…

Through the tumultuous pain radiating from his bashed apart wrists and ankles, Brandon stared in petrified awe at the monolithic monstrosity looming in front of him.

Hardware Tony magnanimously bowed to the quavering, disheveled, distraught man, inhaling the intoxicating aroma permeating from Brandon's abused body.

It was the death smell. The scent of life slowly dispersing from his body. Brandon was already dead; he just was too clueless to know it yet.

"What we have here," he said, affectionately rubbing the giant apparatus, "is a TW 280PHB WOODCHIPPER. Powered by a Kubota 57hp WG1605 four-cylinder petrol engine, the TW 280PHB woodchipper offers 210mm -- that's 8 inches -- of cutting performance, for serious arboriculture and forestry tasks. Timberwolf's 8" road towable petrol woodchipper is nothing short of outstanding. It is built to tackle the toughest of jobs with minimal maintenance. Bigger and stronger, yet still easy to use, the TW 280PHB has an extra-wide feed funnel and open top section to provide better visibility and is bigger in overall area than the nearest rival. Designed with the operator in mind, whether it's additional safety controls -- such as the reverse feed rollers to override the stop bar, or the carefully positioned air filter intakes to draw in cool, dust-free air -- it's up for just about anything you care to throw at it. The devil really is in the details on this beauty!"

Brandon gaped at him, totally thunderstruck.

Tony laughed. "… Sorry, I do sound like a spokesperson for these guys, don't I? But I really love their products! Sure wouldn't say no to an endorsement deal!"

Brandon shook his head crazily. The guy was nothing more than a blue-collared, white trash, overweight, Patrick Bateman, rambling on and on about his implements of hell instead of tailored suits or the best Whitney Houston album.

This mental picture caused Brandon to utter a brittle, raspy chuckle that teetered towards madness. Tony smacked him upside the head a few times, presumably to bring him back to his senses, then shocked him senseless with a jolt from a stun-gun.

***

As Brandon slumped, temporarily relieved of his mental faculties, Tony unlocked the shackles and violently heaved the inert body feet first into the woodchipper's gaping maw. He pushed Brandon down as far as he would go, really stuffing him in there, cramming his feet against the serrated jaws of the vicious machinery.

Then, he stood back and waited for Brandon to come out of his stupor, eager to see his reaction.

Groaning as he revived, Brandon gazed blearily about, and then balked in terror. The amount of panic radiating from him was *gargantuan* … a truly underused word, but clearly the most apt adjective for his frightening predicament, as far as Tony was concerned.

He fired her up, causing a plume of black smoke to belch forth from its exhaust pipe as it rumbled to deafening life and its churning, saw-toothed gears began to grind.

Brandon screeched like hell, his frantic, scrabbling movements almost comical as he jerked his legs up, tucking his knees toward his belly and trying to keep his feet clear of instant destruction. "FUCK!!!! FUCK!!!! FFF-UUU-CCC-KKK!!!!!!!!"

"Look at me, Brandon!" Tony commanded.

Despite his dire situation, Brandon met the gaze of the man -- monster, to him; maestro, to Tony himself -- who had devised and created this hellish scenario. Brandon's eyes burned in hatred like a thousand infernos, pure vitriol streaming from every pore.

Tony, gently but firmly, settled his big hands onto Brandon's shoulders and began to apply a strong and steady downward push.

Brandon strained valiantly, but his vigor had depleted to a point where it was nearly non-existent. His feet touched the blades, mulched into a mushy goop in a split-second, His lower extremities followed suit, masticated and avulsed -- on the bright side, he could no longer cry about his broken ankles, but Tony rather doubted he'd see it that way.

Blood fountained as if from a ruptured water main. Ribbons of muscle, strands of sinew, and torrents of puréed flesh erupted from the discharge chute, jetting a geyser of gore all the way across the warehouse. Fragments of Brandon's leg bones, crunched up into a pulverized spray of bone gravel, followed suit, larger bits peppering the walls like machine gun bullets.

The machine continued to suck him in like a colossal, starved beast slurping up fettuccine alfredo with ferocious hunger. Brandon's arms, busted wrists, and half-flensed hands clawed for any purchase to prevent him from sliding further into the slavering apparatus of death. He also pummeled Tony, hoping to pry loose his grasp or put him down for the count.

On his best day, he would have been hard pressed against Tony's sizable strength. And today was not Brandon's best day… far from it. He gave up striking Tony in favor of seizing the control bar, seeking to forestall the inevitable. His tortured gaze sought the heavens, as if there was an answer, or salvation, hidden somewhere above. But there was only the warehouse ceiling, with no clues hidden in the rafters for him to decipher. There were no solutions to be found.

The only outcome was death, pure and simple.

No matter how tightly he clung to the bar, despite the agony of his shattered wrists, the pull of the woodchipper was relentless, and his palms were too slick with blood to maintain a good hold. The next parts of him to be consumed were his genitals. Brandon hit an even higher octave than AJ had as his testicles were reduced to little more than the pulp found floating in orange juice, his gonads mashed into nothing more than a bloody, fleshy slop. His flaccid penis, snagged into the whirring blades, was degloved much more effectively than his attempts to do the same to his hands, leaving only a raw and twitching, glistening meat stick … before that, too, was milled into liquid hamburger meat and blasted through the chute along with everything else, coating the room in a thin layer of greasy gore.

***

By then, Brandon had screamed so much that his voice could only produce a hoarse whistling. Veins pulsed madly in his head and neck as his body was put through the unending gauntlet of pain. His grip on the bar loosened, and some dim part of him wondered why he was even still bothering to hold on.

The surrounding world faded from his mind and sight, taking on a ghostly white affect. For a moment, he let himself speculate if he was on his way to Heaven or not, but he knew deep in his heart he was not worthy of the pearly gates. Which left only one other destination ...

A sudden silence fell, and at first Brandon thought he really had died. Then he realized it had been the woodchipper's engine shutting down, causing the massive wall of sound to fade. All he could hear now was the copious dripping of blood and meaty droplets plopping everywhere. He weakly looked up, expecting to see that the machine had broken down, or Hardware Tony had inadvertently turned it off, but it seemed he'd done it deliberately, coolly returning Brandon's gaze.

The pain was like a living, breathing thing, mauling him with its razor sharp, needle-like fangs. It was so intense, could not explain the anguish he was going through in any meaningful way; he truly believed there were no words created yet that could describe it properly or with full justice.

"Why ... did ... you ... stop?" Brandon whimpered.

Why was he even still alive? Why hadn't he bled out? It felt as if every part of him from the waist down had been annihilated; he certainly should have bled out! Unless the incredible pressure of the machinery somehow constricted his blood flow, pinching shut the veins and arteries like a giant industrial tourniquet.

Or, maybe he *was* dead, and in Hell, and this was to be his eternity. To be ground up forever in this fucking woodchipper, while a demon with Hardware Tony's face mocked and jeered at him.

Seeing him thoughtfully purse his lips, it sure seemed like the real Tony. "Two reasons, I guess," he mused. "The first is, I want to watch the light fade from your eyes as I collect your soul. I think The Zodiac was right about that ... when you kill someone, you in essence, collecting souls to enslave in the afterlife."

"And ... the other reason?" Brandon gasped.

"Well ... what do you know about air compressors?"

Chapter 16

Under Pressure

Brandon did, in fact, know a little bit about air compressors. Enough to recognize that the one Hardware Tony had was the biggest he'd ever seen, a regular behemoth, dwarfing any other.

"This beauty right here," Tony said, patting the hulking machine like it was a good dog, "is a Mako 5409HBA-E3 scuba SCBA paintball compressor 6000 PSI 33 CFM 3 Phase. One of the most powerful made. It weighs nearly 1300 pounds! Most compressors have a max PSI of 150; this goes to 6,000!"

"You ... still sound like ... a damn salesman," Brandon groaned.

"Well, shoot, you know there's nothing I like better than explaining my tools! Now, a lot of people don't realize how dangerous air compressors can be! Even grown men who ought to know better get up to horseplay. Imagine, there you are at the garage, working on fixing a flat or something, and one of your buddies thinks it'd be funny to point the air compressor hose right at your face and give you a *pffft*. Just a harmless prank, right?"

Brandon felt himself fading out again and greeted the sensation with more relief than dread. Anything to be done with this fucking infomercial. But then, Tony's voice, raised to a hectoring shout, snapped him alert again.

"WRONG! DEAD WRONG!"

Instinctively recoiling was not only a useless gesture; it woke up his pain all over again too.

"Compressed air utilizes *intense* pressure," Tony lectured. "Even that *pffft* can rupture eyeballs or eardrums, split the skin, force air *under* the skin, or into a blood vessel, resulting in an embolism. That's an air pocket inside the body, by the way, and if it reaches the brain or the heart, it can cause a stroke or cardiac arrest. And that's with as little as 12 pounds of air pressure! This bad boy right here, as I said, goes to 6000! These things pack one hell of a wallop!"

Brandon's mind was still sharp enough to understand where this barrage of information was heading. He wished he would just *die* already but the woodchipper really was acting as a kind of tourniquet for his lower half, its vise-like grip serving as a 'tightened belt' cinching off further blood loss.

In other words, whatever fantastical new torture he was about to endure, he would be alive for it. How long he'd stay that way, though, was still a mystery.

Tony unspooled the air compressor hose toward Brandon, cheerily whistling, *"Zip-a-Dee-Doo-Dah,"* from that old Disney film, *"Song of The South,"* sung by the Uncle Remus character; the movie had been banned -- and rightfully so -- for its racist aesthetics.

"Now, this," he declared, holding up a roll of broad heavy-looking white tape, "isn't your ordinary duct tape, no sir! Gorilla Tape is 3x stronger, for a hold that truly lasts. Made with double-thick adhesive, strong reinforced backing, and a tough all-weather shell, it's great for projects and repairs both indoors and out. Gorilla tape sticks to smooth, rough, and uneven surfaces, including wood, stone, stucco, brick, metal and vinyl!"

Brandon groaned again; wasn't the physical torture enough?

Tony prodded at his downcast chin, making him lift his head to give his full, undivided, attention.

"Here's what we are going to do," he said. "I am going to put the end of this hose into your mouth and Gorilla-tape it in place so you can't spit it out. Then, why, then we'll see what happens. I've never tried this before, so I am kinda jazzed to find out … how about you? No? Well, that makes one of us, anyway!"

Though Brandon tried to keep his mouth shut, it was no use. Tony jabbed the hose halfway down his throat, striking his uvula painfully in the process, then wrapped the extremely sticky Gorilla tape around and around until his entire face was practically mummified. It was so tightly wound that Brandon could only make vague, whimpering, muffled sounds of protest.

"Ready?"

He tearfully shook his head "*no*," knowing fully well that the loony toons tool tyrant could care less.

Sure enough, Tony gleefully chanted, "Tough titty said the kitty!" and threw the switch.

Pressurized air shot into Brandon's mouth, the results immediate and graphic. Brandon's cheeks and throat inflated grotesquely. His eardrums popped like blown tires. His eyes bulged out of their sockets like the scene in *Total Recall*, wildly distorting his vision, before spectacularly detonating, blasting twin jets of grimy gore. Ocular tissue, optic nerves, blood, cartilage, and other sludge belched out in a surge.

Blinded, deafened, Brandon tried to scream, but the force of the compressed air surging down his trachea was on a one-way trip, already turning his lungs into balloons fit for the Macy's Thanksgiving Day Parade. It also blasted down his esophagus, spasming his diaphragm and distending his stomach. He could have sworn he felt his forehead swelling, the bone of his skull expanding to the breaking point.

His cheeks split open, blood-misted air hissing out through the rents in his skin and the seams of the overlapping mask of tape. More spouted from his nostrils, his nose also deforming as his sinuses failed to contain the incredible pressure.

Whether his lungs or his head exploded first, he'd never know.

***

Later, Tony was glad the live feed had filmed it, so he could replay this moment over and over again, in slow-motion.

The way Brandon's compromised cranium surged and shifted, like tectonic plates during a violent quake, like some hideous creature was tunneling its way around in there ... surged and shifted and strained and swelled, then split apart and shattered ... not even Tony himself had ever witnessed such a spectacle. A point-blank blast from a twelve-gauge shotgun would have had nothing on this sheer cataclysmic destruction. Blood, clots of brain tissue, chunks of bone, and a slurry of avulsed flesh burst from every crack and orifice.

Gore welled up from the ragged wreckage, a vomitous bulimic hemorrhage.

The released hose whipped back and forth in a crazy out of control frenzy, reminiscent of one of those blow-up tube figures they had at used car lots caught in a tornado. With, Tony noted as he shut the air compressor down, a hefty wedge of Brandon's chin and jawbone still securely Gorilla-taped to the end. That stuff really held like the dickens. He'd have to write a letter to the company.

With all that said and done, just for the hell of it, Tony then turned on the woodchipper again, letting it mangle and mash the rest of the dead man's decapitated cadaver into a pile of steaming, sickening dilapidated flesh.

***

Grinning from the sated satisfaction of a job well done, Tony went around to every section of the warehouse, revisiting every corpse. He used his battered and aged Polaroid camera to take up-close and personal, grisly photos showcasing his work.

The photos were not for him, of course. They were for Rossario Lochiano, who would want to verify that the victims had suffered in unfathomable agony, even the children. Which, of course, had been handled in spades by Tony's estimation. Still, the old Don wanted irrefutable proof, and Tony was fine with providing the old timer some ultra gnarly snuff pics for him to peruse at his leisure.

He had also provided the link for the streaming live feed, courtesy of the surveillance cameras mounted throughout the building. But Rossario was old school, and Tony knew that the old mobster would appreciate these mangled mementos even more than a video he probably couldn't even figure out how to watch. Tony made sure to snap some extra-lurid shots of the women, especially their gore-caked genitals and hacked up tits.

After the Polaroids developed, he placed them into a large manila envelope for safe keeping. He then stripped down, rinsed off, put on cleanish coveralls, and went to his office. There, he sat down heavily in his tattered desk chair, a loud *whooshing* sound escaping from a rip in its side as he did so.

What a day! He was beat, but in a good way, and quite extraordinarily pleased with himself. Even by his standards, this had been one for the record books!

He called the local business he used to clean up after his "art exhibits," as he liked to christen them. They, of course, were mobbed up, so there was no need to give a false story or fear any police repercussions whatsoever.

The phone trilled for three rings before a brusque voice answered the line.

"Yeah, this is Bobby!"

"Hey Bobby; how are you doing, you son of a bitch? It's Tony!"

"Hey Hardware, how's tricks?"

"I'm all tricked out; I had a big night. One of the biggest! That's why I'm calling, actually."

"How many we talkin' about?" Bobby asked.

"Eight large!"

"Damn, you did have yourself a big night!"

"Yup! So, I need your guys to mosey on over here and

clean this place till it sparkles… I got another job lined up for tomorrow!"

"Damn, no shit?" Bobby said.

"No shit."

"Is it from the same crew?"

"Nah, Cifarretto. Bunch of his bitches been bleedin' him dry of funds."

"Marone! That's a lot of dead quim!" Bobby laughed.

"Tell me about it!" Tony snorted.

"Alright, I'll have a crew out there within the hour."

"Sounds fantastic. Thanks Bobby; have a good night!"

"Yeah, you too, Hardware!"

After Tony hung up, he reached into his desk drawer and brought out a brand new Macanudo cigar and used a cigar cutter to snip the head off before lighting it with a match. *Only heathens use a lighter on these babies*, Tony thought smugly as he puffed happily on the smoldering stogie, sending a pungent plume of tobacco smoke into the air.

He leaned back as far as he could in his office chair and used the remote on his desk to power up the small TV mounted on the far wall. A rerun of *Diff'rent Strokes* was on TV Land. It was Tony's favorite episode, a two-parter entitled 'The Bicycle Man,' the one where Arnold and Dudley got kidnapped by a child molester. Tony appreciated it because the episode alluded to Dudley's molestation at the end by the old man.

Arnold had just got done saying his patented line, "What'choo talkin' 'bout, Willis?"

The laugh track erupted in faux mirth from a nonexistent

studio audience. Tony guffawed in delight. He loved when Arnold said his endearing catchphrase… it never got old.

"What indeed, Arnold, what indeed!" Tony chuckled as he tapped a pillar of ashes into a filthy, congested ashtray.

Epilogue

Rossario Lochiano hunched over his luxurious, expansive mahogany wooden desk, the photos from Hardware Tony littering every inch of its surface.

The focal point of his interest was the XXX titillating photos of Meadow and Adriana Rossi. The sight of the two ladies' blood drenched pussies and obliterated tits and assholes had proven an intoxicating fountain of youth for the Don.

His pants and boxers were snaked on the floor around his feet as he frantically jerked on his liver-spotted uncut prick. A mass of gray pubic hairs fettered out around his cringy cock like a bevy of spiders nesting in a basement. Rossario's arthritis-afflicted, gnarled hand whipped his erection with wild abandon as he fantasized about the two dead bitches.

He loved how badly the Ricci's and Rossi's had suffered. Hardware Tony was worth every damned penny.

His carpal tunnel got the better of his dominant hand, making him have to switch out. The sensation of his other hand tugging on his root was almost akin to a stranger's touch instead of his own; it felt foreign, which was admittedly exciting.

He had meant to take a Cialis pill, but the sight of blood and death had rendered the medication unnecessary. His feeble old schlong hadn't been this hard in … twenty years, he supposed, give or take a year or two. Rosie Palm and her five sisters were giving his piss pump the good old "knuckle shuffle," as he liked to call it.

He would need to finish soon, though. Numerous skin tags along the length of his pencil-thin cock were beginning to rip open and weep blood onto his old gray balls, which hung so low it was almost comical. Strands of sparse nut hairs protruded from his mangy ball bag in an erratic fashion, like the shitty goatees that adolescent boys tend to grow in their early teens.

The need to evacuate his ancient baby batter from his smegma infused dick slit struck him with a fierce urgency. When he could hold it at bay no longer, Rossario released a gush of yellowish, stringy cum that looked more like someone suffering from a bad case of the flu had just sneezed all over their hand. His spunk was speckled with unhealthy-looking globs of greenish pus or phlegm, mingling with the alarming, jaundice-colored seminal fluid leaking from his uncircumcised cock like a trickling garden hose.

"WOW! Now that was a dandy nut! Just what the doctor ordered!" He cleaned himself up with a handful of tissues before pulling up his boxers and pants, then tucked all the Polaroids back into their large manila envelope.

Rossario finally felt vindicated for the untimely death of his beautiful daughter Nancy, and her unborn child. A lot had been stripped away from him that night, but with the help of Hardware Tony, he had turned the hands of brutal justice back to his favor.

Let this be a lesson to people, if you mess with the bull, you get the horns, Rossario thought to himself smugly.

The word spread quickly about the mass murder of the two families, and the reasoning behind it. A renewed respect had been bestowed upon Rossario's sagging shoulders, inundating him with some much-needed credibility. People were flabbergasted to find that the old gangster still had it in him to be so devilish, even after all of these years. It filled him with a sense of machismo he hadn't felt since his youth.

It had also apparently amplified his once dormant libido back to fruition, which was utterly amazing in and of itself. In fact, Rossario soon felt it was time to flog the bishop again, going through the grisly crime scene photos and selecting Charmaine Ricci this time around. The chainsaw really had done a number on her pussy, mulching it into a meaty mash, but not so much that it distracted him from being able to have another go.

"One more," he told himself, "and I'll call it a night."

He re-dropped trou, revealing his rock-solid, albeit absurdly bent and wrinkly, cock. But, as he went to grab the lotion, he found it empty, leaving him in a horny quandary. What would he use to slather the one-eyed monster with now?

Without any other immediate option, Rossario hacked up a gray, lumpy loogie tinted with a strange black substance from deep within the recesses of his antique lungs, and aggressively slathered his cock with the suspect slop. He cast his famished eyes back at the dazzling array of gory erotica, particularly the masticated, broken, delicious female flesh.

That chainsaw blade looked to be jammed at least twelve inches up the shredded meat that was all that remained of the woman's ravaged cunt.

Sweat cascaded down his reddening face as he furiously masturbated like a horny teenager with a tattered, dog-eared *Hustler* magazine. Nothing was going to stop him from milking his prehistoric cock until he sprayed another smattering of curdled cum all over his lap.

He had never felt more alive than he did right now, at this precise moment in time. More so than in all the years he had roamed this Earth. Anger truly was a gift. As was cold, cruel revenge.

His seminal fluids erupted from his aching testicles once more, as his body shook from another mind-altering orgasm. His hips bucked wildly as he blasted the desk with his virulent load. Then Rossario flopped tiredly back into his expensive, plush, leather chair, breathing heavily from his abundant carnality.

He thought how far he had come, in his long, illustrious life. How he had risen. He had started off as a penniless immigrant child with nothing but ambition to his name, and now look at him. Power and wealth most people could only dream of! He could have whatever he wanted, have someone killed with a snap of his fingers. The United States truly was the land of opportunity.

"God Bless America!"

As he rose and cleaned himself up once more, he smiled at the collection of photos in all their attractive abhorrence. He had no doubt that he would sleep better tonight than he had in years. Perhaps he would even dream about Meadow's beautiful, mutilated body. He had never fancied himself as a necrophile before, but her maimed cadaver had really gotten his mojo rising! Maybe he could put in a call to Tony before bed and have her body left at the facility... that way he could plumb Meadow's deteriorated depths with his ancient fuck stick in the morning? Rossario quickly picked up his phone and made a call to Hardware and squared away that bit of business before it was too late. Tony, genial as always, Assured the aged mob boss that Meadow's curvaceous cadaver would be waiting for him whenever he was ready to plunder her tasty twat.

An amalgamation of destroyed, nude, female corpses pirouetted in his misogynistic mind as he headed off to bed. None more so than the doomed daughters though. Rossario felt like a child on Christmas eve knowing that Santa was going to deliver the present he desperately wanted.

Yes sir, he told himself, *newborn babies won't slumber as happily or soundly as I will tonight! And just think, I have tomorrow to look forward to! I can do what I want to her body! Afterall, nothing is off-limits to a corpse!*

Afterword

Hello, dear Maggot Colony! Thanks so much for picking up *My Vice Is Your Unfathomable Agony* and giving it a read, I truly hope you enjoyed the wanton depravity in this putrid publication! It was a damned marathon of mutilation and murder at the end, huh?

This story was originally intended to be a part of a 10-day challenge that fell through because of several unforeseen circumstances. Judith, Brian, Christy, and I planned to put a pin in it and come back to it at a later date, when everyone was 100% but something called out to me about this story, commanding me to work on it right away.

It was weird; I have never had a story do that to me before. I had a set number of kills in this that I wanted, and I knew that would make the book longer than the maximum word count allowed for the challenge, which was 18K. This came in at over 30K!

This was also initially going to be my first splatter crimes entry, but I chose to do "Medusa's Son" for that instead, because the story could be leaner, and I could fit everything into the tight confinements of the challenge. *Vice*, I discovered, had a bit more moving parts than I originally anticipated …

This one had quite a bit of buildup and character development before we dove into the atrocious avalanche of gore. My goal was to kind of establish and escalate, before my gauntlet of merciless mutilations pummeled the reader senseless, Hopefully, I attained that!

I've always been fascinated with mobster films, and that

lifestyle in general. My second stepfather was mob affiliated, and he got blinded during a bank heist job where he was shot in the face. He was a huge piece of shit that treated me like garbage; I wish I could've dropped *his* punk-ass at Hardware Tony's slaughter factory ... but, I digress!

You can add films like *Goodfellas, The Godfather Trilogy,* and *Casino* to the list as well. But probably my favorite mafioso masterpiece is *The Sopranos.* I love everything about that HBO series, and I have watched it easily over six times already. Readers with a passing interest in the exploits of Tony Soprano and his two crazy families should be able to sift out some fun Easter eggs littered throughout this crazy ass story.

Another aspect of this story that I thought was important was the killings. I wanted gnarly kills, of course; after all, it's what I do! But I wanted to use non-typical weapons that you wouldn't normally find in a story like this.

A few weeks back, I was in Home Depot, and as anyone can attest that's been inside one of these monolithic buildings, you know how easy it is to get lost in the fucking place! So, there I was, wandering around aimlessly, searching for the one thing I had come in there for, when I kept seeing all these various tools in the aisles that could really be used to murder people in exciting and gory fashions! I was astounded, to be honest. And that's all it took to get the ball rolling; the story quickly started to take hold in my pea-sized brain.

I thought, *what if a mobster hitman only used tools from, like, a hardware store to kill his victims?*

And, just like magic, Hardware Tony came alive in my mind!

I found an employee who could direct me to the item I

needed to purchase, paid for said item, and then hurried home to start plotting out this tale of violent retribution. I perused the internet and found the various tools I wanted to play a part in this book. Some weapons were obvious, while others were not so much. I had a lot of fun plotting all the myriad ways the Rossi and Ricci families bit the dust, and I hope you had fun reading the results!

It is surreal that September is over, and October is officially here! This year has just flown by! What a crazy year so far. With the death of my mother and then the passing of my wife's grandmother, it's been hard emotionally for me and my family. But the writing was always there to take my mind away from the pain, and "save me," I guess you could say.

Writing is truly a form of magic. Anyone who has tried to become a writer can attest to that fact. Not everyone can do it; being able to mentally will the words to fall into place for an author to tell a (hopefully) entertaining story to their wonderful readers is no easy feat, let me tell you! I feel blessed that I have been able to make the magic work for me. Will   it always be there? Only time will tell, but for now, I am happy to say I seemingly have unlimited amounts of ideas that should translate into compelling, ultra-violent books to push the boundaries of extreme horror.

Finding the time to pen them? Well, that's another problem in and of itself, LOL.

Next, I am jumping headfirst into the deranged world of *No One Rides for Free (Absolute Chaos)*, with the one and only Judith Sonnet! This is very exciting for me because it'll be an entirely new experience. A true collaboration on a single story where both authors work on it is something I have been dying to try out. And my first time is with one of my best friends and literary idols to boot! I plan to horrify readers with my special take on Buster and The Man's penchant for depravity and viciousness and crank that fucker up to 11!

As for the rest of the year, or what's left of it, I would love to squeak out one last project, but I am unsure if time is on my side for that one. It's going to be another collaboration of short stories with a writer that I not only admire but get to call a friend as well. It will harken back to the old EC comics like *Tales from The Crypt, The Vault of Horror,* and *The Haunt of Fear,* but with all of the ample gore and sexual perversions extreme horror fans love and clamor for! I'll talk more about this project as it gathers more steam.

And, I don't know about you guys, but I've been missing my girl Morticia lately. I wonder what she's been up to. Maybe we can find out next year together…

Thanks again for taking the time to purchase and read an Otis Bateman book. My fans are some of the sweetest people out there! I love receiving messages from everyone regarding my work, checking on me, giving me a good-natured hard time, or just sending me positive vibes. I've also had two fans plan on getting Maggot Girl tattoos! I, of course, am humbled by all of this. I really lucked out with you all, so thank you from the bottom of my blackened heart for giving me a platform to try and entertain you! Till we meet again, stay gory!

XoXo
Otis Bateman
Grandview Missouri
10/14/2023

Books by Otis Bateman

Maggot Girl Episode 1: A Maggoty
Metamorphosis

Maggot Girl Episode 2: Snuff Porn Holocaust

Maggot Girl Episode 3: Denouncement of
Depravity

I Simply Am Not There

Medusa's Son: Splatter Crimes

Cerberus

Evil Rose Up: Splatter At Sea

Dino Gore

My Vice Is Your Unfathomable Agony

Printed in Great Britain
by Amazon